NIGHT BEACH

ALSO BY JOANNE DEMAIO

The Seaside Saga
Blue Jeans and Coffee Beans
The Denim Blue Sea
Beach Blues
Beach Breeze
The Beach Inn
Beach Bliss
Castaway Cottage
Night Beach
Little Beach Bungalow
Every Summer
—And More Seaside Saga Books—

Summer Standalone Novels
True Blend
Whole Latte Life

Winter Novels
Eighteen Winters
First Flurries
Cardinal Cabin
Snow Deer and Cocoa Cheer
Snowflakes and Coffee Cakes

night beach

A NOVEL

JOANNE DEMAIO

This is a work of fiction. Names, characters, places, and incidents are either the product of the author's imagination or are used fictitiously. Any resemblance to actual persons, living or dead, events, or locales is entirely coincidental.

No part of this book may be reproduced, or stored in a retrieval system, or transmitted in any form or by any means, electronic, mechanical, photocopying, recording, or otherwise, now known or hereinafter invented, without express written permission of the copyright owner.

Copyright © 2019 Joanne DeMaio
All rights reserved.

ISBN: 9781790577071

www.joannedemaio.com

*To my daughter Mary,
for photographing the night beach with me.*

Beautiful inspiration for this story.

one

9:30 p.m. – Saturday

NEVER TURN YOUR BACK ON *the sea.*

Jason Barlow remembers his father's long-ago words. They often carried some life parallel. Those words hit him hard as he sees the sad remnants of the seaside vow renewal ceremony that never came to pass.

The ceremony that, so close to becoming a beautiful sunset reality, was cancelled.

From Jason's vantage point in the last-standing cottage on the beach, it's all he thinks as he looks out the salt-coated porch window onto this troubled night. *Never turn your back on the sea.* Moonlight wavers on the rippling Long Island Sound.

His father was right. As calm as that moonlit water might look, it's as treacherous, too. Just like the framed photograph hanging on the Fenwicks' porch. Jason glances over at the picture. In it, a monster storm wave towers over

Stony Point Beach during a hurricane decades ago. That wave, reaching up from the sea, claimed any cottages and lives within its dangerous reach.

Which is exactly how this night feels. Dangerous.

The wave of one person, of Shane Bradford, reached over Stony Point today when no one was looking. When their backs were turned. Now, everyone's fighting to regain their footing—to not be taken down by that man's presence.

Putting up the strongest fight is Shane's brother, Kyle. Kyle Bradford, tonight's groom—who never even made it into his tailored suit. His pale gray vest and pants still hang in Jason's house, where he was supposed to get ready for the vow renewal ceremony. Where Kyle was supposed to have a ham grinder and cold beer out on Jason's deck. Where Jason, as his best man, would toast Kyle and Lauren's next ten years of marriage after surviving the first tumultuous decade.

Instead, upon learning of Shane's arrival, Kyle called off the vow renewal and disappeared for hours. An all-out search ensued to find him. To calm him down. To make sure he was okay. Which Jason eventually did when he found him upset on the beach.

Now, Jason sees how Kyle still wears the wrinkled tee and cargo shorts he'd put on first thing in the morning that seems days ago. His hair is messed, his posture tired. Even more telling, Kyle's unusually quiet on the Fenwicks' porch. He sits in a faded wicker chair and drinks a hot coffee simply to get his bearings. But he says nothing, even as

Mitch offers him some words, and as Carol, Mitch's daughter, opens kitchen cabinets and pulls out dishes and cups.

Because what can Kyle say when his world fell apart? The night was supposed to be all about love. And celebration. Kyle and Lauren together, dancing beneath the light of the nearly full moon.

Now that moon shines on all that went wrong.

Even from the cottage window, Jason can make out the distant boat basin, misty in the moonlight. He knows a rowboat is decorated with flowers there. Wedding flowers. White roses nestled in greens had been tucked into the boat's bow. The little wooden vessel was meant to carry Lauren to her vow renewal ceremony on the sand.

That never happened.

The decorated rowboat is still docked and waiting; the bride, devastated elsewhere. Jason only hopes someone's helping her through the night, too.

Still standing at the porch window, Jason turns when Mitch approaches. And Jason's got to hand it to Mitch Fenwick, a client and acquaintance really, for reaching out tonight. When he invited Jason and an inebriated Kyle into his cottage-on-the-sand so they'd have a quiet place to regroup, it was Jason's small miracle. Now Mitch stops beside Jason and looks out the window toward the sea.

"This beach isn't big enough for the two of them," Jason tells Mitch.

"For the two of them?" Mitch glances over at the defeated groom. "For Kyle? And his brother, Shane?"

"Yeah. Maybe for the three of us."

Jason can't help it then. At the mere mention of Shane being Kyle's brother, he recalls the times Kyle has told him, *You're like the brother I never had, Barlow.* He'd said it while competing to be Jason's best man; while bullshitting over a beer on hot summer evenings at The Sand Bar; tonight, even. That's how deep the rift grew between Kyle and Shane over the years. It stopped them from being brothers.

"Hell, maybe Stony Point isn't big enough for everybody," Jason adds while dragging his father's Vietnam War dog tags along their silver chain. "Damn beach is getting smaller and smaller with each new arrival."

"Or maybe it's just a good night gone wrong?"

"No, it's more than that, Mitch." Jason watches out the expansive porch window, where gentle waves roll onto the sand across the night beach. Those waves break in a silver froth beneath the moonlight.

Mitch's voice is quiet beside him. "Just how bad of a guy is this Shane? Because any brother of Kyle's, well … Kyle's all right. A good man with a big heart, so—"

"It's not that Shane's a bad guy." Jason looks at Mitch, then at Kyle in his wicker chair—still a wreck, still downing coffee from a mug. "It's just that where Shane Bradford goes, so goes trouble."

two

9:45 p.m. – Saturday

TWICE IN KYLE BRADFORD'S LIFE, he almost stumbled to his death. Being a former union steelworker, this was surprising. Because after years of shipbuilding work that had him perched high on precarious scaffolding, he'd always been one thing: sure on his feet.

Ah, but life, cruel life, sometimes did the trick.

Ten years have passed since the first near-fatal stumble. It was the night, just weeks before his wedding, when Lauren left him for Neil Barlow. When she set Kyle's diamond engagement ring on his pickup's dashboard and ended things—right there, parked at the curb. Later that night, Kyle argued with Neil. In the midst of their heated words hitting like shrapnel, Kyle tripped in the dark and almost went over the rocky bluff at the Barlow house, down into crashing breaking waves.

The second stumble came a few summers ago when

Kyle's life hit the skids, job-wise and marriage-wise. After crying the blues to Jason and Matt, a few drinks and a careless attitude found Kyle walking the top rail of the boardwalk's seatback. His balance wavered that dark night, and he nearly took a fatal fall onto the boat basin's concrete landing twenty feet below.

Twice, stumbled.

Twice, a Barlow brother was there to pull him back.

Because his own brother, after all, was dead to him.

Kyle has this thought as he fumbles with the Fenwicks' cottage slider, before stumbling onto the elevated deck outside.

Yes, he knows a thing or two about falling. Tonight, it feels like he's falling again. The difference this time is that there's no helping hand to break that fall.

Leaning against the white deck rails alone, he looks out at the nearly full moon hanging low over the water. That moon means one thing. The day has ended—and in a way he never saw coming. When Kyle turns and looks down the length of the beach, the depressing evidence is there: the empty floating dock close to shore; the remaining vacant guest chairs still waiting to be folded and stacked; the lit tiki torches flickering on the sand. Further down the beach, lamplight spills from the cottages up on the hill. Folks are inside, or on their decks overlooking the Sound. He's sure that ice clinks in cool drinks, talk is animated, easy laughter rises.

Everywhere but here.

Looking again at the partially cleared white chairs, all

Kyle knows is that he can't look at this night beach much longer. It taunts him with visions of what should have been. In the lacy breaking waves, he sees the lace of Lauren's two-piece wedding dress—her long fitted skirt clinging close, the sleeveless top revealing a hint of bare midriff. In the rhythmic splash of those waves, Kyle hears the melody of Celia's guitar serenading his and Lauren's first sandy dance. In the touch of salty sea damp on the deck rails, he feels the salty touch of happy tears on Lauren's face. In the sweet scent of the sea carried on a soft breeze, he smells the sweet scent of wine as crystal goblets are raised in a celebratory toast to their renewed vows.

Problem is, none of it happened.

All of it was stopped cold with the arrival of his estranged brother.

When the slider screen scrapes open behind him, Carol Fenwick steps out. If Kyle had to guess, he'd say she's in her early thirties. She wears a gauzy kimono over a tank top and ripped jeans. Her hair is bobbed in a blunt cut, and long bangs sweep her eyes. Glancing at her, Kyle is grateful for one thing: that she doesn't know his *entire* pathetic life story—only tonight's crappy chapter.

"I brought you a snack," Carol says.

Right. If you'd call a feast a snack. Kyle walks over as she sets a deluxe turkey club, dill pickle, potato salad and more coffee on the patio table, then pulls out his chair.

"Here. Eat," she orders him. "You need to get some food in you. On top of everything else, you don't want a killer hangover tomorrow."

"Thanks." Kyle sits at the table and slides the heaping plate closer. He lifts a sandwich half, then sets it down again.

"Go on," Carol says, nudging over another dish. "The potato salad's homemade, from a cookout we had earlier."

Kyle tastes a loaded forkful and gives her a thumbs-up while chewing.

Standing in the shadows, Carol lights a lantern on the table. "You don't know me, Kyle," she says as the lantern light flickers. "But if you want to talk, well, my unbiased ear is good at listening."

Kyle lifts his sandwich again, but pauses. "It's just that something went down with my brother today." He bites into the turkey club and wipes his chin with a napkin. "He showed up at Stony Point after being gone for fifteen years."

"Wow." Carol sits in a chair across from him. "Now that's a long time gone."

Kyle nods while chewing. The sandwich, with its tangy dressing, is extraordinarily good. Was he really this hungry? Did he even eat today? He takes another bite, then says around the food, "My brother and I had words ages ago. Those fifteen years, to be exact. And the words? They were pretty damn harsh. It was around the time my father died." He glances out at that floating dock where Lauren was supposed to arrive by rowboat for their vow renewal ceremony. Shaking his head, he looks back at Carol. "We drifted apart after that."

"I have a brother." Carol moves the lantern to the side.

"He lives in the Pacific Northwest. I couldn't imagine not talking to him."

Well. What can Kyle even say to that? You never imagine these things will happen. You grow up thinking you've got a bro for life. A ready-made best man. Godfather to your children. Until the unimaginable *does* happen.

So Kyle says nothing, and instead takes another hefty bite of that double-decker turkey club on toast.

"You must've thought about him over the years, no?" Carol asks. "Shane, is it?"

"Here and there." What Kyle doesn't say is that recently those thoughts came as he lowered a taper to a candlewick in church. Some mornings, he swung in on his way to work. With sudden sadness, he lit a candle for Shane, then blessed himself and hurried out. "Shane's my kid brother, a couple years younger than me," he only says.

"Kyle. You seem like a nice guy. You helped us out getting my grandfather Gordon's towboat off of Little Beach. You're Jason's friend." She pauses, leans close and clasps his arm. "Want me to go get Shane for you?"

"What?"

"No. Hear me out." Carol gives his arm a shake before sitting back and eyeing him in the lantern light. "There's no one around here. Jason's leaving to clean things up on the beach, so it'll just be me and my dad inside. And what if ten minutes alone with Shane could fix things? How about if that's all it takes? You never know. So I'll get him ... if you want."

In her pause, waves lap at shore just below the deck of

this cottage-on-stilts. Over and over, that rhythm of the sea reaches Kyle. It's like the water is whispering to him with the splash of that lapping. *No, no, no*, over and over again.

So he shakes his head, silently—sure of his answer.

"Picture it, though, before you decide," Carol persists. "You know. The two of you can sit right here beside the sea, on this very deck. Talk. Have a beer. Because what if that works?"

When Kyle stops eating and sits back, arms crossed, Carol crosses hers, too. Her insistence comes naturally. He sees it in the steady way her eyes hold his, in her subtle nod that doesn't want to take his no for an answer.

"What if ten minutes with your brother helps fix things with your *wife*?" she whispers.

Beyond the cottage deck, those white wedding chairs that were never filled with guests still need to be taken down. The floating dock that Lauren never arrived at via rowboat still glimmers in the moonlight. Tiki torches still throw wavering shadows on the sand. Empty sand that should have been danced on tonight.

Could the day *really* get any worse having Shane here for a few minutes? Kyle weighs that thought. Again, he shakes his head at Carol.

"No?" she asks. "You're *sure*? Because I can go to the inn and get him, no problem."

"No." Kyle takes a long breath of the sea air. "No, Carol. I'd rather you not."

three

10:00 p.m. – Saturday

CLIFF RAINES IS ON ONE mission and one mission only: get himself to the Ocean Star Inn, pronto. When he'd told Jason an hour ago that Elsa was putting on coffee for Shane, Jason wouldn't stand for it and let Cliff know. In no uncertain terms.

You go tell Elsa to pour that coffee down the fucking drain and get that Shane out of there. Now!

Then, according to the next words Jason tossed his way, Cliff was to throw his commissioner weight around and order Shane Bradford out of the inn and effectively out of all their lives.

There's no time to explain, Jason went on. *But trust me on this one, Cliff. Your loyalty needs to be to Kyle tonight.*

The thing is? Cliff owes it to Jason to not let him down. Not Jason, of all people, who's guarding Cliff's own secret—that *he's* actually little Sailor, the mysterious boy rescued during a hurricane here fifty years ago. The boy for whom another man, Gordon, lost his life. So off Cliff went, half-walking, half-jogging the sandy beach roads toward Elsa's inn, intent on accomplishing his mission.

And everything in Stony Point is standing in his way.

Starting with the fact that someone removed all the speed barriers on a busy, cottage-lined road so that the weekend traffic can zip back and forth. Which, Cliff notes, it is doing. Much too quickly.

"For Pete's sake," he mutters while looking first in one direction, then the other. The wood-framed barriers are set back on cottage lawns now.

The real question is: Who moved the sawhorse-like gates? Because if nothing else, he'd like to issue that person a serious fine for jeopardizing vacationers' safety.

Instead all Cliff can do is drag the wooden barriers back onto the street, one at a time, strategically placed for traffic control. The fifteen-mile-per-hour speed limit is intended to match the laid-back, charming feel of the bungalows and cottages nestled here. Nice and easy does it.

Just another reason to set up more security cameras, Cliff thinks while aligning one of the speed barriers across half the street. But some residents here see cameras as an invasion of their privacy.

"Hogwash," he says to himself. Because what about some poor kid getting hit by a car chock-full of boxes and suitcases, the vehicle speeding slapdash to a cottage in some manic vacation-anticipation? Where are the priorities?

Beneath the misty light of the streetlamps, Cliff finally lugs the last speed barriers into place, one on this side, the other on that. As he finishes and resumes his trek to Elsa's, he can make out her inn a few blocks down. An old, unfamiliar pickup truck is parked in the driveway. He squints in the low light to decipher the model, or license plate details. Because there's only one person that weather-beaten vehicle can belong to—Shane Bradford. Which means he's still there at Elsa's inn. So Cliff picks up his pace, first veering off in the direction of his trailer to get his COMMISSIONER cap and jacket. Any sign of authority might help him evict this Shane fellow.

"Commissioner!" a voice calls out a block later. A man, waving his arm, runs into the street. "Come quick! Big problem over here." The man grabs Cliff and pulls him around the side of a silver bungalow with a large loft addition. Behind the back porch, the man points out a lidded garbage can—and the can's actually moving.

"Mercy!" Cliff says.

"There's an animal in it," the breathless man explains. "A raccoon. It got up on our porch railing, reached down and pulled open the can lid, then dove right in."

"Have you called animal control?"

"No."

Cliff looks over his shoulder to see a woman with small children watching from the porch. "Get the children away!" he shouts while pulling his cell phone from his pocket. "And do *not* open that bin."

The harried man who flagged him down picks up an old

straw broom and hovers in the yard. He looks ready to swing that broom and defend house and home should the wild creature emerge from the lidded can. Lidded and still moving.

Raccoon or not, as Cliff dials animal control, he has only one thought. If he doesn't get to Elsa's inn and get Shane out of there, Jason Barlow will be indignant. *Indignant.*

"You say you've received several calls tonight?" Cliff asks into his cell phone moments later. He throws one last, longing glance in the direction of the Ocean Star Inn, where there's a fresh pot of coffee needing to be tossed down the drain. Oh, he can see the drama of it—his grabbing the pot and dumping it, Elsa's astonishment at his brazenness, and of course he can just imagine Jason's grateful pat on the shoulder afterward.

If Cliff can ever get there on time.

Instead he listens to the equally exasperated animal control dispatcher bemoaning the raccoon and skunk population of these cottage communities. As the dispatcher starts to explain how the animals have gotten bolder in recent years, Cliff abruptly cuts him off.

"Well, just how long do I have to wait for assistance?"

Elsa DeLuca never imagined that her very first guest at the Ocean Star Inn would be hated.

But as innkeeper, it's not her place to judge. Her intent was always to open the grand cottage's doors to any weary traveler seeking shelter from life's seas.

And Shane Bradford is no exception.

So when she hears him come down the stairs a little after ten, then hears him heading to the hall toward the front door, she calls out from the kitchen. "Shane?"

In a moment, Shane walks into the room. "Elsa." He turns up his hands and looks around. "What's up?"

"Shane." After setting her coffee carafe and two mugs on a tray, she adds a plate of biscotti before turning to him. He wears a lightweight button-down over a dark tank and jeans, with that cotton newsboy cap on as though he's headed out. "Are you going somewhere?"

"Just for a walk down the beach. Clear my thoughts."

"Care to join me on the terrace first? I've got fresh decaf."

"Me? Well ... I don't want to keep you up, Elsa."

"Nonsense. It's only ten o'clock. The night is young. Come on."

"Allow me, then," Shane says while taking the tray and following Elsa out the kitchen's side door.

They walk over to one of the inn's wood-planked bistro tables scattered on the terrace. As Shane sets the coffee cups on the table, Elsa's chilly in her black lacy jumpsuit. So she hurries back inside for her cropped cardigan to keep the sea damp off her shoulders. When she returns, she also brings a clear Mason jar containing a tea-light candle set in golden sand. In her other hand, she holds an uncooked strand of spaghetti and a book of matches.

"Would you mind?" she asks, handing Shane the

matches. When he strikes a match, she extends the spaghetti strand for him to light its tip. Once the flame takes, she dips the burning spaghetti tip into the Mason jar to light the silver candle nestled in sand.

"Interesting way to light a candle," Shane says as he removes his cap and sets it aside.

"Your brother taught me this trick. Don't have to worry about burning your fingers this way." Elsa glances over at Shane while putting the illuminated jar near their coffee. "Kyle's good with trivia like that," she adds, sitting at the planked table that's already been stripped of its white linen. Beside a nearby stone walkway, the August dune grasses are long and sweeping. They rustle in the sea breeze; and in the moonlight, she can make out the hidden path through them to the beach. Beyond, out of sight from their table, Long Island Sound's gentle waves lap at shore. She loves listening to them at night, when all else is still. Her son, Salvatore, listened to the waves, too. She'd catch him sitting out here often, quiet, facing the distant sea.

It's that thought that moves her now. Because though Elsa knows everyone is *devastated* by Shane's presence, and has insinuated he's no good, she feels differently. Shane is her first guest, after all, and has been nothing but polite. Not to mention, Sal would turn over in his grave if she didn't offer Shane hospitality at her new seaside inn.

"What a day," she begins with the candle burning between them. She lifts the coffee carafe and fills both cups, adding cream to hers. "I spent the evening overseeing the caterers. Except instead of serving dinner, they folded up all the tables and took down the white tent."

"It's a shame everything ended that way," Shane says. He lifts his coffee cup for a sip.

"It is. And I'm not saying this with antagonism, Shane. Or malice. Just with concern. You must figure the day fell apart because of your being here?"

"Which wasn't my intent, Elsa. I *was* invited, and so I thought Kyle was good with it."

Elsa, sipping her coffee, shakes her head.

An annoyed breath, then, from her mysterious guest. "Did he even know I was invited?" Shane asks.

"No."

"You mean, Lauren didn't *tell* Kyle she invited me?"

Elsa hesitates when she hears Shane become defensive. "You know something? Never mind all that," she says while waving away their words. "I may have overstepped a boundary bringing this up, and it's not my place. It's just that I'm close with everyone here."

"I get it." Shane leans back in his chair and glances out toward the water before continuing. "We protect the ones we love."

Elsa nods. "But let's set all that aside and start fresh, if I may." She extends her hand across the bistro table. "Thank you for coming to the Ocean Star Inn, Shane." What surprises her is the way he takes her hand in both of his then. As he does, she sees several tattoos extending beyond his cuffed shirtsleeve. And when he gives her hand a small squeeze, she knows—all is forgiven. Fresh start granted. "I hope you're enjoying your stay so far," she tells him. "The best you can, at least. You are my first unofficial guest, you know."

"It's a beautiful place you've got here." He motions to the grand three-story inn, with its cedar-shingled turret and open porches. Starfish are propped in the lamplit, paned windows; a rock wall borders the yard; a line of white Adirondack chairs sits on the far lawn, facing the sea. "When do you *officially* open for business?"

"Soon. Labor Day weekend. And this," she says, nudging the candlelit Mason jar, "is one of the inn's signature features."

"This jar?" Shane picks it up and runs his fingers over the glass while looking at the seashells set around the candle inside. The flame flickers, and the sand beneath it sparkles in the candlelight.

"Oh, it's not *just* a jar. It's a happiness jar. You'll see them throughout the inn. My niece made some of these two years ago for her wedding. *Happiness* jars, she called them, as she filled them with beach sand and seashells, and ribbons and dried flowers and special keepsakes from her wedding. I liked the idea of that … to bottle pieces of happiness whenever we find them."

"Nice."

"I thought so, too. So I incorporated the jars into the décor here for my guests to fill with happy memories. There's one in your room. Be sure to fill it and take it with you when you leave."

"Thanks, but I've already got plenty of Stony Point memories."

Memories, Elsa thinks, noticing how he left out the word *happy*. As she takes a lemon-almond biscotti, Shane reaches into his pocket and pulls out a smooth stone.

"It's a skimming stone," he says when he notices her watching. "Whenever I see a good one, I pick it up."

"Oh! From the beach here?"

"No." He flips the stone in the air, then catches it. "I took a ride over to the docks on Shore Road earlier. Walked around and found it there." He lightly drops the skimming stone beside the flickering candle in her Mason jar. "I'll add it to *your* happiness jar."

"So skimming stones bring happy memories for you, then?" While asking, she slides the plate of biscotti his way.

After a quiet moment, as though Shane's deliberating something—weighing it, gauging it—he takes a long breath of the night's salty air. "Me and my brother had some intense skimming competitions, back in the day."

Elsa dunks her biscotti into her coffee and smiles. "That's a start," she admits, dipping, dipping again, then biting into the biscotti. "We have some time and the coffee's hot. So, Shane Bradford." She leans back, her hand around her coffee cup. "Tell me something more about yourself."

four

10:30 p.m. – Saturday

FRIENDSHIP IS ONE THING.

And Mitch Fenwick's proven to Jason he's a friend tonight, taking Kyle in for a few hours to pull himself together.

But patience is another.

And if Jason doesn't get the vow renewal detritus off the beach *and* get Kyle on his way soon, Mitch's patience is sure to wear thin.

So after leaving Kyle at the Fenwicks' for another coffee, Jason headed to the beach alone. As Kyle's best man, he owes him this much. Owes Kyle a beach cleared of any regretted memories; of any embarrassment; of any of those telltale white chairs. But before he starts folding them up, Jason grabs a minute to check in with his wife.

"Where are you now?" he says into his phone. Beyond the dune grasses in front of the bench where he sits, he sees the dark silhouette of a couple taking a late beach walk.

"I first stopped home and changed out of my dress. Now I'm at Eva's," Maris answers.

"I thought you two were headed to Lauren's."

"We are. But we got sidetracked when my sister's nurturing instinct kicked in, big time. You know how she gets. She made some food for Lauren to freeze. A plate of chicken cutlets, side of penne."

"Classic Eva." Jason looks further down the night beach, where the white chairs and wedding decorations remain untouched. The sight of it brings him his own panic. He's got to get the damn beach cleared—once and for all. "Listen. Can you do me a favor?"

"Anything, babe."

"When you see Lauren, tell her I found Kyle?"

"Seriously? You found him? Where?"

"Wait," Eva's voice comes through, too, right as some pot or pan falls into the sink beneath running water. "Kyle's back? Oh my God. Is he with Lauren?"

"Hang on," Jason tells Maris. "Tell your sister to slow it *way* down. Kyle's here, but he's upset and needs some time." While Maris fills in Eva, Jason looks toward the Fenwick cottage on the sand, where Kyle's got only another hour or so to get his shit together before Jason returns for him.

"Do you think he'll go home to Lauren tonight?" Maris asks.

"Not sure. But listen, you're breaking up, sweetheart." Jason stands and walks a few steps toward the beach. "Just tell Lauren I found him. And it would really help if you could call off the search for me, too. Let everyone know Kyle's safe and okay. Call Matt and Vinny—they're looking for him at the casinos. And Nick, who I think is actually out on his Whaler, searching along the coast. Maybe even text Elsa and Cliff—who should be at the inn right about now, evicting Shane from the premises."

"I'm a lobsterman."

"A lobsterman?" Sitting at the bistro table, Elsa squints through the shadows at Shane. He's a big guy, with his light brown hair cut short, a trace of whiskers on his face. And there are those tattoos. But none of those explain some change that came over him once he sat at their small table overlooking the beach. Is this why he seems most comfortable right *here*, outside near the water? Because he's a lobsterman, at home on the sea?

"For almost twenty years now," Shane goes on as he reaches for a chocolate-glazed biscotti, which he dunks into his coffee. "I live in Maine, and work out of Rockport."

"That's *right*. You mentioned you came down the coast to get here." The candle flickers in the Mason jar between them; the night is dark beyond it. "Now this is just fascinating to me," Elsa admits while lifting the carafe and topping off her coffee cup. "So. A lobsterman ... which means you spend your time on boats, out on the ocean?"

"Gone about ten months out of the year," he says around

a mouthful of the coffee-soaked pastry. "Sometimes it's as much as two weeks on the boat, off for a few days, then right back out for another two weeks."

"And what do you do, exactly?"

"I'm a crewman. Pretty much the captain's right-hand man. Which means when the traps come up, I get the lobsters out of them, measure and band them. When the trap's empty, I skewer a handful of herring or pogies, rebait the trap and stack it on the stern. Captain drops it in the water wherever he decides it needs to be."

Shane's voice is quiet, Elsa notices. But intent. He chooses his words carefully, and frugally. She imagines this is how he might work on deck, too. Efficiently.

"It can be pretty routine," Shane explains. "Almost like an assembly line, the way the same things get done over and over again. Traps in, emptied. Lobsters measured and banded, traps rebaited. Every day. Day in and day out."

"So you know what to expect when you board the boats."

Shane gives a small laugh. "The *responsibilities* are routine. But the sea? Far from it. And that's the challenge of my livelihood. When you're miles offshore, the waters get temperamental, and they damn well let you know it. From twenty-foot waves tossed my way to ice-coated decks to the wind whipping up a frenzy of salt water on real dirty days, the Atlantic has put me to the test."

"You're a working man, then."

"I am. I work the sea."

"Which is a hard life, I'd imagine."

"And you'd be right, Elsa. Sometimes I love it, other times ... not so much. But it's all I know."

"So what drew you to it?"

"Well, that's the thing." Shane folds his hands together on the table. "I didn't *choose* this life. More like it chose me."

"Really. How so?"

"I was just a kid in high school, my first time out lobstering." He pauses, taking a long sip of his coffee. "A contentious kid in and out of trouble, and I guess I needed to find something big and bad enough to take my attitude. To take the chip on my shoulder. Because I had a rough time, growing up. Our father did the best he could with me and Kyle, after our mother died."

"Oh, I had no idea, and am sorry to hear that."

Shane nods. "But you know, I pushed the limits. So I saw the inside of a few detention centers. A few courtrooms. Until a couple of things straightened me out. A girlfriend, back in the day."

"And the sea, I'm guessing?"

"Absolutely. At seventeen, instead of another stint in juvie, I was assigned to a mentor on my first lobster boat. Kind of as a community service thing when I'd crossed the law one too many times. And let me tell you. That chip on my shoulder?" He clasps his hands behind his neck, leans back and glances toward the beach through Elsa's secret path. "The Atlantic Ocean wasted no time knocking it straight off and putting me in my rightful place."

five

10:40 p.m. — Saturday

IT SEEMS LIKE JASON'S BEEN snapping white chairs closed all night.

He hasn't, though. Instead he *planned* to, earlier, when he was on the boardwalk with Cliff. Made good on that plan, too. Once Cliff left to clear Shane out of Elsa's inn, Jason walked toward those white chairs on the sand. Beneath the moonlight, those empty chairs haunted the night beach. Who couldn't help but think of what should've been? Who wouldn't picture those chairs filled with ethereal spirits waiting for a seaside ceremony? In the misty glow, the sight was downright eerie.

And Jason *did* close some of the chairs earlier. He snapped a few shut and tossed them aside. Until his task was sidelined by Kyle and an hour in the Fenwick cottage.

So, yes, it seems like those chairs have been an eternal part of the evening—from seeing them, planning to close them, getting some done, and still seeing them now. Mid-snap of a chair, he's surprised when Carol Fenwick approaches to give him a hand. Beyond, her family's cottage rises in shadow from the sand, with Kyle and Mitch still inside.

"How's Kyle doing?" Jason asks.

"Okay. He had a sandwich, coffee. We talked on the deck."

"I don't know if he might've been more riled up than liquored up tonight," Jason says as he snaps another chair shut. "Maybe a little of both. But I really appreciate how you and Mitch helped out."

"What now for Kyle?" Carol asks when she lifts a chair.

"Don't know." Jason glances toward the cottage-on-stilts. "We can't seem to get beyond this one night." As he says it, he drags a chair closer and sits with a long, salt-air breath. In, and out. He's tired, and his leg's acting up again with some nagging phantom pain. Just a little, in his missing foot. A pins-and-needles sensation has come and gone all night. So it feels good to take the weight off his prosthesis. Would help if he could get out of these wedding threads, too, and into something more comfortable. He unbuttons his gray vest and takes another long breath.

"Do you need something?" Carol asks. "Aspirin, maybe? Or a drink from the cottage?"

"I'll be all right. It's been a long day and I'm just going to take five." He sits back in the white chair and looks out at the night. Tiny stars fill the sky over the sea, and that low-slung moon has a way of casting long, vague shadows on the beach. As the night goes on, a salty breeze lifts off the Sound and slightly cools the air. "This weather is exactly like one night, a long time ago," Jason says, more to himself than to Carol. So much about the beach right now reminds him of that night.

"Ah, yes, Mr. Barlow." Carol adds a folded chair to the stack. "Beach memories. They're like a mirage, don't you think? Misty around the edges, unclear."

"Sometimes. Tonight, though? This one memory's crystal clear. The whole gang was there, on the night I'm thinking of."

"Back when you were kids?"

"Kids? Hell, no. Old enough to know exactly what we were doing."

When he glances at Carol, she brings a chair beside his, faces the sea, sits and listens. "Tell me about it," she softly says.

Jason looks long at her beside him, then drags his hand through his hair, remembering. That same salty breeze as then touches his face; the waves break just as easy. "Must be fifteen years ago now," he begins. "That's about when the rift between Kyle and his brother all began."

That particular night didn't start as a Shane thing, Jason admits to Carol. *It was just a summer bonfire with all the old friends on Little Beach. A reunion, after we'd not seen each other, not been together since the summer before. We were all in our early twenties then, and figured we'd bullshit, have a beer, see what everyone was up to.*

"Yo, I've got the hooch," Vinny called out when he and Paige emerged from the woods. Paige shone a flashlight across the beach until the beam landed on us guys. The moon hung low, and in its light, me, my brother, Kyle and Matt had dug a firepit in the sand and loaded it with dried seaweed and twigs.

"Crack that shit open, Vincenzo," Kyle told him. "And it better be good stuff." Kyle reached for a larger piece of driftwood from a pile of tree branches and wood scraps. Carefully, he and I crisscrossed kindling, then set heavier pieces of wood on top.

While Vinny splashed the liquor into red cups, Paige dispensed a cup to everyone—including Maris and Eva, who'd just walked off the wooded path onto the night beach.

"Hey, hey," Lauren said while looking over at Maris and Eva before eyeing me and Matt standing the teepee logs around the woodpile. Wearing an ankle-length gypsy skirt, Lauren gave a twirl on the sand, arms outstretched, her skirt spinning. "The gang's all here."

"Just like old times," Maris agreed, right as Neil lit the kindling and the fire took hold.

Eva held her red cup to the sky in a summer toast. "Let the party begin."

The thing is, once everyone was there, the night took on a different feel. It wasn't like old times. This wasn't a night like when we were teenagers.

No, tonight was different. Because first of all, our teen years were behind us—in age, in life. Now, Eva and Matt's daughter was practically two years old. My sister, Paige, and Vinny were engaged to be married. Maris graduated college a few months earlier. And me and Neil were working together, getting Barlow Architecture off the ground.

Teenagers? Far from it.

And then, of course, the gang wasn't all there. I knew it, and I figured everyone else did, too.

But no one was saying so.

No one was saying that one certain friend was missing at this summer reunion. Shane Bradford, with his easy smile and devil-may-care attitude, was glaringly absent. He wouldn't be there to get us going with one of his harmonica jams; to challenge his brother to a night swim; to show where he'd been inked or to compare scars with.

Surprisingly, the one to finally mention Shane—and even then, only once we were half lit—was Kyle.

I can see it still, Jason says to Carol after a long pause. He throws a glance in the direction of Little Beach beyond the dark patch of woods. *All of it,* he continues.

Kyle, kneeling close to the light of the fire as he wrote something on several pieces of paper. Swaying a little as he put pen to pad.

Flames licking the night sky; brilliant sparks rising to that sky like spinning stars.

Lauren, slowly circling the roaring bonfire and giving each of us one of the paper scraps.

Kyle, standing then. Paper in one hand, alcohol in the other. His face was lined with perspiration that night; his hair damp.

Eva and Matt, sitting in the sand and leaning into each other near the cooler.

Maris, standing off to the side, sipping her drink and watching Kyle. Her hair was long and in a loose braid; her jeans faded.

Paige and Vinny sitting with me and Neil; Paige opening a bag of marshmallows as Vinny held a waiting twig.

But everyone stopped with Kyle's words. His emotional talk hinted at how his brother wronged him, had crossed a line of ethics in one of the most reckless acts Shane had ever committed. One that stung Kyle deeply. We all knew the story, and we all felt for Kyle.

"After Shane and I had it out after my father's funeral, well, I'm here to announce beneath this rising moon that Shane Bradford's no longer my brother. Not in any way that could matter to me," Kyle said. "So each of you are holding a piece of paper with Shane's name on it."

The motion caught my eye then, of the friends glancing at the papers their fingers clutched.

"After the stunt Shane pulled, we're done. My vow, sealed here tonight, is to never speak of Shane Bradford again. To never utter his name."

In one solemn moment, Kyle stepped to the roaring bonfire and tossed his paper into the flames. Lauren was first to follow, murmuring her vow to never say Shane's name again; Vinny, next, nodded in agreement as he tossed his paper into the flames; then Paige, and Eva. My brother? Well, Neil tried. He asked Kyle if he was sure about this. When Kyle just crossed those arms of his and squinted at my brother in the light of that fire, Neil turned up his hands and circled the bonfire pit. Matt stood, too, clasping Kyle's shoulder before he gave an underhand toss and his paper looped through the air into the fire. I joined him, saluting Kyle as I crumpled Shane's name and flung it deep into the flickering flames. We'd all backed Kyle; half lit, we all vowed into those flames right along with him. Everyone except Neil, that is.

The only one left was Maris. When I went to her standing in the shadows, I saw what no one else did. I saw the way her hand quickly swiped away tears before she stepped out of the darkness. Before she took hesitant steps toward the fire.

The night had really turned potent. What we were doing, as adults, meant something. And Maris? Well, I knew. Somehow, I knew. Her steps weren't hesitant because she might be looped from the liquor. It was something else—not the second and third cup everyone was working on and holding up in a paused toast as Maris approached the fire.

With all eyes on her, I stayed by her side. My arm was around her waist when she turned back and looked at Kyle. Then—I could never be sure, though—I swore Maris whispered, "Goodbye, Shane," before pulling her paper from her sweatshirt pocket and tossing the folded note into the fire.

———

Jason stands then and snaps his white chair closed. But Carol doesn't. Watching him in disbelief, she's still sitting on her chair.

"And you *agreed?*" Carol asks. "All of you agreed to never utter Shane's name again?"

"We did."

"Doesn't that seem extreme? Or cruel, even?"

Jason gives a regretful sigh. "You don't understand, Carol. We form alliances. We were a tight group of beach friends. And you know, Shane really wronged his brother. Hell, I had a brother."

"Neil. So he was still alive then?"

Jason nods. "And Neil never would've *wronged* me like that. That's not to say we always saw eye to eye on things. That's different. But a brother? Well. Brothers are loyal. There's a certain code between them."

"And whatever Shane did, he broke the code."

"You could say that. So, yeah. Sitting around the fire that night, I agreed. I wrote him off."

"And all these years later, no one's making even a *mention* of what Shane did?"

"Honestly, Carol? That's Shane and Kyle's story to tell." Jason picks up his folded chair and heads to the waiting stack. "And it's a long story, for another night," he says over his shoulder. "Let's get through cleaning up the mess of this one, first."

Carol relents and brings her chair to the stack, too. As the rows of white folding chairs are simply erased, the beach returns to some semblance of normalcy. Finally there are only the vow-renewal signs, orange cones and flip-flop baskets left in the light of glimmering tiki torches.

"I've got these, Carol. Thanks for your help, though. Truly appreciated." Jason picks up an armful of the vow-renewal pointer signs that Lauren painted onto old boardwalk planks. "I'll load this into Cliff's golf cart and drop it all off in his supply shed."

"Are you coming back?" Carol asks while lifting beach hydrangeas off the last of a few decorative roped dock posts.

"You bet. Let your father know I won't be long, would

you? I'll get Kyle on his way."

As Jason crosses the sand then, that rising moon shines a swath of silver across the rippling water, straight to shore where the small waves lap, over and over. Jason glances back toward the woods beyond the Fenwick cottage. The woods where a narrow, winding path leads to Little Beach on the other side of tall oaks and pines.

Fifteen years have passed since that bonfire burned. Since they all got caught up in a moment on a hot summer night and tossed Shane Bradford's name into flames licking at the sky.

And it worked. Son of a bitch, it worked. No one spoke of the man since. They moved on, lived their lives and acclimated to his absence.

For God's sake, that bonfire was like a funeral pyre, if Jason had to say so. It laid to rest all they knew of Shane Bradford in those damn flames.

But doesn't Jason know it now—don't they all—that some small spark always smoldered beneath the embers.

six

11:00 p.m. – Saturday

A WHITE CHANDELIER HANGS ABOVE the white-painted dining room table in the Fenwick cottage. The chairs are white, too, with navy plaid cushions. Kyle sits on one of those chairs; Mitch sits beside him. Coffee cups are in front of them both. The chandelier is only dimly lit so as not to interfere with their view through a large window. That window looks out onto the night Sound. Its water is as dark as the sky, except for where the heavy moon shines across it, illuminating the big rock and swim raft.

"It was going to be real nice, Mitch. It's our ten-year anniversary, and me and Lauren were going to do it up big, starting with the vow renewal. We even rented a cabin near a lake for a few days," Kyle says. "For our second honeymoon."

"That right? Whereabouts?"

"Addison."

"Addison? Right here in Connecticut?"

"Sure is."

"Well, that's close enough."

"Would've been. But it's empty now, that cabin. Waiting, like everything was waiting today. I'll have to call Gus, the guy who owns the place, and cancel. I'm sure I'll have to pay a cancellation fee, but whatever. That honeymoon's not going to happen."

"Hang on." Mitch pulls over a serving plate of half-eaten cheesecake. "Don't make critical decisions yet. Let's think about this over another slice." He divvies up the cheesecake and gets the coffeepot from the kitchen to freshen their coffee, too. "Because listen, Kyle," Mitch says while topping off Kyle's cup. "Sometimes a cabin in the woods is just what a man needs. I like to tell my students that sometimes."

"Your students? Do you teach high school?"

"No. I'm an English professor at the college a couple of towns over. My students are always taken by Henry David Thoreau's account of living in a cabin in the woods. Of living *deliberately*. And in a way, Kyle, maybe a little empty cabin can help you, too."

"You think?"

"Well sure," Mitch calls out while returning the coffeepot to the kitchen. "Worked nicely for Thoreau," he adds when he sits beside Kyle again.

"You know, I heard about that dude." Kyle forks a hunk of the strawberry-laden cheesecake. "Spent a couple of years in the woods, right?"

"He certainly did. At Walden Pond in Massachusetts.

Spent the hours writing. Thinking. Paring life down to what matters. So you're *not* to cancel your cabin reservation, you hear?"

Kyle looks at Mitch beside him. His graying blond hair is pulled back in a small ponytail; his short-sleeve button-down and khakis are wrinkled at day's end. And he's drawing his hand over his goatee while contemplating something.

"Just go with me on this, Kyle."

"Wait a sec, Professor." Kyle spears another piece of cheesecake. "Thoreau, being literary and all and living in a cabin, is one thing," he tells Mitch. "Not really sure a cabin will solve *my* problems, though. This is more a family issue, and my marriage is on the line, too."

"But you'll never think straight in the place that broke your heart … here at Stony Point. Take advantage of that cabin. And its lake. You'll have clarity there." Mitch pauses and sips his coffee while facing the sea beyond the window. "Look. My wife, Kate, she's been dead five years now. And it pains me to see you and *your* wife split up like this. So come on, son." Mitch suddenly stands, stealing one last mouthful of cheesecake as he does. "Addison's not far. I'll bring you to that cabin," he says around the food.

"No, Mitch. You've done enough already." Kyle wipes his mouth with a napkin and stands, too. "And anyway, the drive there will do me good. It's only about forty minutes from here."

Mitch carefully eyes him in the shadowy room.

"I'm better now," Kyle reassures him. "Had some chow,

and a few coffees brought me right down. I'll get some air on the beach first. I'll be okay."

"Well what about your bride? Lauren? You taking her, too?"

"No. I'm going to use that Thoreau *solitude*, like you said." Kyle pushes in his chair. "If Lauren should call, or comes looking for me, you can tell her that. Yeah." The more he thinks about it, the more the idea grows on Kyle. He heads toward the slider to the deck. "Yeah. I'll be at the cabin in the woods."

"Where's your vehicle?"

"Behind your place. Champion Road turnaround."

Mitch walks over to Kyle. "But are you really okay to drive, man? No shittin' me now."

"Hell, yeah. I've been here a couple hours. Like I said, I'll walk the beach first, breathe that sweet salt air before I leave. Maybe catch Jason, too. Tell him my plans." Kyle opens the slider screen, rusty on its tracks, then turns back to Mitch behind him. "I'm good, Mitch. Really," he says, extending his hand for a shake before hurrying down the deck stairs to the sand.

In fact, Kyle's feeling good enough to skip the beach walk. Instead, he just takes a few long breaths as he circles around the Fenwick cottage to the street running behind it.

By the time Kyle gets to his truck on Champion Road, he hopes Mitch is right. Hopes a cabin in the woods will give him clarity.

Because by the time he drives the beach roads and passes beneath the stone train trestle, he's finding it hard to take a full breath again, not with visions of a distraught Lauren coming to mind.

And by the time he's cruising Shore Road, every doubt of every decision he's made today comes back to haunt him—from his angry words telling Lauren he can't stand with her on the sand, to his insistence on canning the vow renewal, to his ditched plan to catch up with Barlow somewhere on the beach. Kyle's caught in a crossfire of his own panicked thoughts. Those doubts keep coming at him just like the wind whipping in his open truck window.

Once on the highway to Addison, traffic is light and he tries to let go of some of his worry. Long stretches of pavement lie in front of him with not another car's taillights in sight. More obvious, though, is how behind him, the sea's already diminished into nothing. No salt air is to be had here on the highway. No muffled foghorn wails. No lapping waves splashing onshore.

No cancelled event, disappointed friends, devastated bride.

It's just Kyle and the scrubby grasses roadside, the forests rising beyond.

"*Thoreau*," he whispers, both hands on the wheel as he leans close to the windshield, the broken lines of the highway skimming past.

Finally. Yes, *finally* Cliff closes up the steel entry door of the Stony Point Beach Association's trailer. The same trailer

Cliff also secretly calls home. Standing on the top step outside, he pulls on his official COMMISSIONER cap—black with gold stitching—then zips his COMMISSIONER windbreaker, too.

Done. He's minutes away from emptying Elsa's coffeepot down the drain and evicting Shane Bradford from the Ocean Star Inn.

Walking down the four metal steps to the small parking lot, Cliff remembers one last thing to do: summon some luck on this ridiculous night when he's been nothing but waylaid. So he pulls his prized scuffed domino from his jacket pocket, tosses and catches it, hoping for luck to be on his side now. Heaven knows he's lost too much time already with those speed blocks first, then with that darn raccoon. It wasn't until the animal control officer tipped the occupied garbage can on its side—and the raccoon lumbered out—that Cliff was free to move on. Quickly now, he adds a note to his phone's reminder app. "*Raccoon preventive tips in next newsletter*," he whispers as he types.

But still, his nerves are fraying. Jason will *kill* him if he catches wind of these delays. And it's already eleven o'clock! Regardless, Cliff figures if he hurries now, he can be at the inn and dumping coffee in no time flat. Once settled in his car—seat-belted in, security walkie-talkie tossed on passenger seat—he peels out of the trailer's gravel lot. Thankfully no one's taking a late-night stroll on his street, where they might have just gotten pelted by the flying stones of his spinning tires.

Spinning tires that come to a screeching halt when that

walkie-talkie ringtone suddenly pierces the silence in his car. Cliff pulls over and answers the call.

"Commissioner! Emergency!" Static as one of the newer security guards pauses, then, "Beached boat alert."

"What?"

"A boat. Beached boat. A sailboat, actually, washed up on the rocks."

"At the end of the beach?"

"No. I was in the guard shack when a call came in about a boat on the bluff. It washed right up onto the rocks."

"Near Barlow's place?"

"No, no. The other end of Sea View Road. And someone could get hurt. Neighbors there are venturing out for a closer look. Already witnessed some tripping and stumbling in the dark."

His walkie-talkie gives a loud chirp as Cliff clicks off and tosses the unit on the passenger seat. "Fiddlesticks," he mumbles while putting his car in gear. After checking the rearview mirror, he does the *only* thing anyone fearing Jason Barlow's wrath would do.

Oh, yes. With the car slightly moving, Cliff yanks the steering wheel all the way, gives the gas full throttle and gets the engine roaring. He's in that much of a hurry.

While smoking his tires and knocking down a speed barrier, too, he does a doughnut.

That's right—a perfectly executed doughnut on the narrow, sandy street. Oh, if only his son, Denny, witnessed this one. Cliff spins the car completely around in a sharp one-eighty before shimmying to a stop.

A stop long enough only to take a disbelieving breath.

In a cloud of smoke then, he heads out in the direction of the beached boat.

And leaves Elsa and Shane and one sorry pot of coffee in his dust.

"I have a great respect for the sea. Which means I never underestimate her power." Shane looks in Long Island Sound's direction beyond the dune grasses. "As beautiful as she can be—and believe me, I've seen ocean sunsets the likes of which no one has—my guard is always up. Especially when I'm offshore. The sea can turn in just a breeze. While we're working the traps, her waves can sweep right over the deck, very willing to take any of us right into the water with their retreat. I've gone in myself a time or two."

"You mean off the boat? Overboard in the middle of the Atlantic?" Elsa asks.

Shane nods. "The boys are right on things, though. They've hauled me out to safety, none the worse for wear. So there's almost a daring audacity that comes when we stand up to the ocean while hauling the traps, doing our job regardless of her moods."

"Maybe still defending some of that chip on your shoulder?" She raises her coffee cup in a toast to his way of life.

"Maybe," Shane admits with a knowing smile, and

raising his cup in return. "Because after a couple days ashore, I'm always ready to go back. There's no better feeling than when I stand on the dock, lift my duffel and throw it up onto the waiting boat. No better sound, either, than that thud when the packed duffel hits the deck."

"Really ... No better sound? Birdsong. Someone special's voice. Oh, I don't know, a concert, maybe?"

"No. Because when that heavy duffel hits the boat's deck, it means I have two weeks ahead of me. Two weeks of being miles out on the water. Sometimes we're as much as a hundred fifty miles from land. No cell phones, no Internet."

"Not too many people could survive like that nowadays."

"We're a dying breed, for sure, us boys on the lobster boats." Shane lightly spins the Mason jar on the table. "It's a very authentic existence out there. Raw, and real, with no terra firma beneath my feet. It's hard to explain, loving the sea the way I do. Especially when she's so indifferent to me, ready to knock me down, to bring me over. But ... she's my life."

Sitting here like this, talking by candlelight in the dark of night, a soft sea breeze reaching them from the beach, Elsa thinks only this: If anyone were to walk in on this conversation with Shane, they'd think he was certainly talking about a woman, and his love for her. Not of the sea.

"Are you married, Shane? Children?"

"No. I came close to marriage once. Didn't work out. Maybe she was somewhat indifferent to me, too. So after that, my second love, the sea, became my first."

"My son would've liked you. Oh, wouldn't he have convinced you to let him try a few days in your shoes. Take the wind on his face, sea spray in his hair. He liked to do that ... try out people's ways of life."

"You say that as though he's gone?"

"He is, my Sal. He left this world a year ago now."

When Shane reaches across the table and simply squeezes Elsa's hand, she's moved to say something more. Something she might not have otherwise said tonight.

"You know, I just don't get it." When she pats his hand on hers, she feels the strength of his working hands, feels the ridge of a scar press against her skin.

"Get what?"

"Everyone here made you out to be someone awful. But after talking to you, I don't get how the day came *undone*." She tips her head, watching him. Seeing his way of cutting to the chase. Of saying things like they are. Of having a certain honesty born from years on the sea, perhaps, and understanding life differently because of it. "I mean, Lauren and Kyle's big event was *cancelled* ... just because of you?"

Shane sits back so that he's partially in the night's shadows now. He's quiet, then sips his coffee. When his voice comes to her, she's actually not surprised by his plainspoken words.

"Tell me about my brother, Elsa. We haven't talked in fifteen years. How's life treating him?"

seven

11:05 p.m. – Saturday

TONIGHT THE TABLES ARE TURNED.

Yet the feeling is so familiar to Celia, this sitting in a quiet room in a house not her own. The windows are open to the night air. Crickets chirp, slowly, as if listening in on the talk. Only last year, it was Celia missing a man not there—Sal—while Lauren puttered in the kitchen, chatting to get her through.

The difference tonight is that it's Celia doing the puttering and chatting to *her* beach friend as Lauren's missing her husband.

"Your kids are with your parents?" Celia asks from the fireplace mantel. She's holding a framed photograph of Evan and Hailey building a sandcastle on the beach.

"My mom said they can stay as long as necessary," Lauren tells her. "She told me they're so sad, though. Kyle taught them some dance moves for the reception, and …

you know. Well, there's no dancing tonight."

"Aw, little Ev and Hailey-copter bustin' a move with Kyle?"

"They practiced so much."

"I'm sure your mom and dad are reassuring them, though. And at least you don't have to worry about your kids being here. Now how about if I reheat some food from the inn?" On her way to Lauren's kitchen, Celia closes a living room window and draws the curtains. "*Mangia, mangia, che ti fa' bene.*"

"Something Sal used to say?" Lauren asks from where she sits on the sofa, her legs curled beneath her.

Celia stops and looks over at Lauren. Gone is the stunning two-piece lace wedding dress. Gone is the perfectly beachy chignon. Gone is the gold band never slipped onto her finger this evening. In their place are frayed denim shorts with a lace-up black silky shirt, an utterly fallen chignon and a bare ring finger. Tears, too. Plenty of those.

Celia can't help it then. She walks over and gives Lauren's shoulder a squeeze. "*Mangia, mangia. Che ti fa' bene,*" she says again in Italian. "Eat, eat. It'll do you good. And Sal firmly believed that."

"I actually reached out to Kyle's brother because of Sal."

"Sal?" Celia straightens the silver maid-of-honor dress she still wears and sits beside her friend.

Lauren nods. "Because of his insistence that second chances were *molto speciale.*"

"Very special."

"Right. And what if our vow renewal could've given

Kyle and Shane a second chance at being brothers? A chance to repair their relationship."

Celia reaches over and tucks a fallen strand of Lauren's blonde hair back into her chignon. "Kyle didn't see it that way?"

"I tried to explain it this afternoon. But he couldn't even hear me beyond his own anger." Lauren gets up and paces the living room, stopping in the open doorway to the front porch. "Believe me, I was as shocked as Kyle to learn Shane actually showed up. When I never got an RSVP, I thought, well, water under the bridge—and dropped it. Didn't even tell Kyle I sent the invite. Now it feels like I pulled the trigger on our marriage."

"Don't say that."

"But what will we do next?" Lauren asks while walking out onto the porch, where twinkly lights line each and every window. She stops and looks out toward the bay. "Put up a *For Sale* sign in front of our beach bungalow? Sell all this? Move?" She pauses only to swipe a tear from her face. "Get divorced and split our time with the kids? Because right now, everything feels irreparable. No one can fix the damage I did."

"I don't believe that," Celia counters from the porch doorway. Arms folded, she leans against the doorjamb. "Not from what I've seen of you and Kyle. You two are so solid and love each other too much."

"Sometimes love isn't enough." Lauren's voice drops, making her quiet words dire. "What you don't realize is that when I sent Shane his invitation, I invited the blackest, baddest sheep right back into the flock."

"Shane?" Celia steps onto the porch. "Shane Bradford? I met him when he checked into the inn. He seems like a nice-enough guy."

"Nice?" Lauren squints through the darkness at Celia. "That's subjective. Because Shane, well, Shane made some bad choices that would have you think—"

Just then, a sudden knock on the outside door makes Lauren jump. And Celia sees it, sees that Lauren wants nothing more than for it to be Kyle standing there. Lauren wouldn't care if he were dejected, mad, upset, or completely confused. It's obvious she would sweep him right in, regardless.

But it's not Kyle. Celia goes and unlocks the screen door for Maris and Eva.

"We brought food and news," Maris says. "Good news."

"Good news?" Lauren asks. "*That* we can definitely use."

Maris rushes in and sits with Lauren on the little porch sofa. "Kyle's okay, Lauren."

"Oh thank God! Where is he?" She looks over at Eva holding some large tote.

"That's the thing. We're not actually sure," Eva admits.

"But Jason called me," Maris explains, "and said Kyle's *with* him and that he's okay. Calming down, and needing some quiet time. But rest assured, Jason *is* with him."

"You really don't know where?"

"No." On her way inside, Eva stops in the living room

doorway. "Jason's cell phone was breaking up," she says over her shoulder. "But I wanted to drop off some fresh tomatoes and chicken cutlets in the meantime. Enough for a few days' dinner, Lauren. With pasta sauce, too, so you guys can have some penne on the side."

"You didn't have to do that, Eva," Lauren tells her from her sofa seat.

"Oh sweetie, it was the least I could do," Eva insists when she steps back onto the porch, carefully bends—tote in hand—and leaves a kiss on Lauren's cheek. "Anyway, it's late and I really can't stay. But you need to eat. So I made sandwiches, too, for right now. I'll bring some out on a platter and put the rest in the fridge."

"I'll help," Celia says, joining Eva in the kitchen. When they soon return to the porch with a spread of chicken sandwiches slathered with mayo and garden tomatoes, along with a bag of organic potato chips and a bottle of wine, Lauren's explaining her twinkly lights to Maris.

"I swore when we first looked at this house, I'd put twinkly lights around the porch windows and I'd turn them on all year." She glances up at the tiny white lights, then presses back a sob. "So it would feel like Christmas every single night," she manages to whisper. "And I did it. I strung them right when we moved in. Remember?"

"Aw, hon. Of course I do," Maris says. "Do you want me to turn them off tonight?"

"No," Lauren says. In a pause, there's the sound of waves lapping at the bay across the street. The night is completely dark now, the sea air wafting in feeling a bit cooler. "Leave them on in case Kyle comes home." She stands again, goes to a window and looks out toward the street. "Those little lights are so pretty, and maybe they'll give him some hope if he sees them."

⁓

The candle in the Mason jar glimmers between them. As the night grows longer, and darker, the candle flame throws wavering shadows. When Shane shifts in his seat and props an elbow on the planked bistro table, that light catches his surprised expression.

"So my brother and his wife actually live *here* at Stony Point now? They have a cottage?"

"A year-round place," Elsa tells him. "A nice bungalow on the bay. They moved in earlier this summer."

"I had no idea. Just assumed Kyle was still in Eastfield."

"No. So many of us drop anchor right here, Shane."

Shane sets down his coffee cup and sits back in shadow. Watching her, he drags a hand across his whiskered jaw. There's a hint of mistrust, maybe, in his pause? Elsa can't be sure, and so she silently waits for his words.

"What brought *you* here, Elsa?" he finally asks. "I don't remember you from the past."

"No, you wouldn't. I've only been at Stony Point two years now. Before that I was living in Italy." She stands then, and walks to the solar landscape lights set among clay pots filled with top-heavy red geraniums, their blossoms lush. One light's post is leaning, though, and she straightens it while explaining. "I'm American, but uprooted to Milan once I graduated college. I'd met an Italian man while studying abroad, married him and raised our son there. After my husband died a few years ago," she says, glancing beyond the dunes toward the sky over the sea, "I reunited with long-lost family members here. And then? Well, then I couldn't bear to leave. And at the same time, this rambling cottage was in complete shambles—*and* on the market."

"The old Foley's place."

"Yes." She makes a sweeping motion to her now-grand inn before sitting at the table again. "It gave me a purpose, at my stage in life—a widow in my late fifties. A *new* purpose … with my husband gone, and my son working and living close by in Manhattan at the time. Yes, I bought this place, which was in such disrepair, let me tell you. And somehow, I managed to transform the big old cottage—and myself, too—in the process." With that, she raises her coffee cup to Shane in a toast.

To which Shane obliges, clinking his mug to hers. "I'd say you did all right." He looks over his shoulder at the inn. "I'd never even recognize the joint now."

"It's special to me. The name is, too."

"Ocean Star Inn."

"Yes. Ocean stars appear on the Sound each morning when sparkling sunlight hits the water. It gives the illusion of stars shining on the sea. I'm sure you've seen them out on the ocean, when the sun rises."

Shane sips his coffee with a nod.

"My sister, years ago, told me that ocean stars are

celestial stars fallen from the night sky. The stars rest on the sea to regain their strength before rising to those same night skies again. Which is why my architect gave me a turret with three levels of windows facing the sea. So my guests can witness the ocean-star phenomenon during their stay here."

Shane stands, steps back onto the expansive lawn and looks up at the illuminated building. When he gives a low whistle, Elsa joins him on the dewy grass and points out the turret. "I'll be hosting Sunday dinners for my guests, too, so the dining room ceiling was raised to accommodate the floor-to-ceiling windows *also* looking out to sea."

Silently, they take in the sight together: the white globe bulbs Cliff strung around the wraparound porch special for today; the wide stone walkway circling the building; the upper deck extending off the turret; the ornamental beach grasses and rock wall; the subdued lighting that has the cedar-shingled structure shimmering in the sea mist.

"Very stunning, Elsa," Shane finally says while slowly walking across the yard, seeming unable to take his eyes off the inn. "I've got lots of memories here."

Elsa's a little thrown. Shane Bradford's been gone from Stony Point for so long, she wouldn't have thought he had memories that might surface, or even matter. "From right here?" she asks.

"Yeah, what a trip." He takes a long breath of the damp sea air. "I don't know how much you're aware of … But like I said, back in the day this place was called Foley's. The big cottage also housed a small grocery store stocking bread and milk and such for the summer renters. The store had a slamming screen door, creaking floors, you know the drill. The family's living quarters were upstairs, and on the back of the store," Shane says, pointing around to the side of the turret, "a local handyman tacked on a good-sized room. Had a jukebox in there, pinball machine. A place for the kids to hang out. Especially—"

"I know. Oh *Marone*, do I *know*!" Elsa says, clasping Shane's arm. Then in a quick, hushed voice, she goes on. "Old man Foley added on the room *especially* for his grandson, a kid rough around the edges." Elsa looks from the turret to Shane standing beside her. "Maybe a little like you?"

"Hey, now," Shane says with a laugh. "Well. Maybe a little."

"And have I got a surprise for you, Shane Bradford." Elsa motions for Shane to follow her inside. "Grab your cap and come with me."

eight

11:20 p.m. – Saturday

THESE AREN'T THE KINDS OF hugs Lauren had counted on today. Celia can tell. These hugs linger. Maris pulls away only to wipe another tear from Lauren's fatigued face. Eva holds *her* hug a little too long.

There are no smiles, either, as Maris and Eva say their goodnights and leave. No one wraps their arms around Lauren and twirls with her, laughing with their beach friend. Or takes Lauren's arms in their hands, steps back and eyes her stunning wedding dress from top to bottom. The wedding dress that's hanging from Lauren's closet door right now—her frayed shorts and black lace-up top on in its place.

"Please, Maris," Lauren calls through the screen door after Maris and Eva walk out to the front yard. "If you happen to run into him, try to get Shane out of here. He'll do anything for you. Always has."

Maris turns and takes a few steps backward. "If I see him, I'll try. But Shane and I haven't talked in so long."

"I know." Barefoot, Lauren steps out into the night and stops on the grass. She crosses her arms against the sea damp. "But still. You meant the world to him once."

Celia sees, too, how after Maris rushes over and gives Lauren one more sad hug, Lauren stays outside. Even after Maris and Eva are out of sight, walking home, Lauren stands there. In a moment, she looks up to the night sky. Celia does, too, from the porch. She sees the smattering of tiny stars against the black velvet night and wonders just what Lauren must be wishing—what last hope is being pleaded to the heavens above.

Once Lauren comes back inside, she sits on the porch sofa. It's a spot where she can catch first sight of Kyle's pickup returning. His headlight beams would round the curve in the road just before the vehicle did.

"Maris used to be with *Shane*?" Celia asks. "The two of them were together?"

"They started going out one summer in high school," Lauren's hushed voice says.

"You're kidding! Hard to picture that."

"It was years ago. Maris would spend two months every summer at Eva's cottage. Shane and Kyle's folks usually rented a cottage on the same street. Long story short? Maris and Shane paired up. Really, it was this *beach* that brought them together. They didn't even live in the same town."

"Huh. Story of all our lives here?"

"Pretty much," Lauren agrees. "Maris and Shane were

still a couple even when she was in college. Which was all way before Maris ever reconnected with Jason."

Celia sits in a wicker chair near an open window. Propped on a distressed white table beside her is a glass fishing float wrapped in strands of jute rope. What strikes Celia is how the friends here are as entwined as that nautical rope weaving this way and that across the green glass globe.

"Shane and Maris broke up right before she finished college, a long time ago now. I never really knew why," Lauren says. "But Shane loved her to pieces." Lauren fidgets with the crisscross fabric at her neckline, dragging her fingers along one of the laces. "Maybe they knew it couldn't work back then, with their polar opposite lives. I mean, when you think about it ... a fashion designer whose boyfriend is a lobsterman?"

"Lobsterman?"

"Mm-hmm. Shane's a commercial lobsterman out of Maine. But before he moved north, he stomped on a lot of hearts here. Maris'. Kyle's." Lauren's fingers still toy with her blouse laces. "I don't know. Was Shane just reckless in his twenties? Is he the same man now?" She shrugs on the dimly lit porch. Twinkling lights glimmer on the window frames; outside, darkness presses against the panes. "No one's talked to him in fifteen years, Kyle included. Not since they had a falling-out after their father died."

"Sounds complicated."

"It is. And I'm just too exhausted to get into *that* story now. But trust me, Cee. It wasn't good. And from what I saw of Kyle today, there's no fixing it." Lauren stands and goes to one of the windows. She leans on the wall beside it and looks out toward the road. "What a long, sad day it's been."

"Anything I can do for you, hon? Stay the night? I'll check on Aria and come back?"

Lauren shakes her head.

"No?" Celia asks.

"I'll touch base with my parents, then wait for Kyle. It's best if it's just me here, if he comes home. I pray to God Jason's getting through to him." Lauren turns to Celia. "But you know what you *can* do?"

"Anything."

Lauren seems to go into some kind of trance then, her words soft and airy as she talks. It's as though she's wishfully living a beautiful moment that never happened. "Instead of walking down an aisle tonight, I was going to arrive at the ceremony in the inn's old wooden rowboat."

As she talks about the white roses decorating the boat, and how Cliff planned to paddle her to shore, Lauren mentions the special shawl she'd wear on the water; the illuminated temporary dock where she'd get out and walk a floating ramp to the beach; how Kyle would be waiting there at Elsa's driftwood podium. The podium where they'd reach for each other's hands and, with Elsa officiating as JP, renew their vows with hope and love.

"The sand would be warm," she nearly whispers. "The sky pink, every white chair filled."

Celia hears the heartbreak at how that moment had come *this* close.

"I'm sure Cliff's gotten to the beach to clean up the decorations," Lauren says now, her voice back to reality. "But I can just picture the sad rowboat docked in the boat basin, completely forgotten. And with all those gorgeous flowers on it." She gives a small smile. "If people see those flowers tomorrow ... well, I don't want to draw any more attention to this awful day. Is there any chance you can clean out that boat on your way home?"

Celia stands, checks the slim silver watch that she put on hours ago to match her fitted silver dress, then hugs Lauren. It's just after eleven—late, but early enough for this one last task which shouldn't take long. Anything to help her true-blue beach friend. "Absolutely," she tells her.

While Lauren's getting some things together, Celia straightens her maid-of-honor dress and slips into a pair of flat sandals Lauren let her borrow. Wearing heels won't cut it in the boat basin, and would only make climbing into an unsteady, floating rowboat dangerous.

In a few minutes, Lauren's back with a thin cardigan sweater. "To cover your shoulders," she whispers while draping it on over Celia's silver dress. "And just stuff the flowers in these," she adds, giving her a few large trash bags and a pair of garden gloves. "There's no sense keeping those roses now. Oh, and one more thing." She hands Celia a small key ring. "Please. Take our golf cart. It's really late, and I don't want you walking the streets alone."

The last-standing cottage on the beach looks like a beacon in the night. As Jason approaches it to pick up Kyle, that moonlit cottage rises on the sand. Mitch Fenwick inviting Kyle inside earlier was a godsend. It gave Kyle a private haven where he could unwind, come down, clear his head.

"I'm here for Kyle," Jason says when he sees Mitch on the outside deck. A lantern flickers on the patio table where he sits. "Beach is all cleaned up, so we'll get out of your hair now."

"Kyle? Didn't he catch up with you? He's gone."

"What do you mean … *gone*?" Jason hurries up the deck stairs. "Gone where?"

"To that little cabin in the woods."

"*What?* But that's all the way in Addison. You think he was okay to drive there?"

"He seemed pretty well sobered up. Had some food, coffee. We talked, Jason. He might've been more upset tonight than anything else. So that cabin's the best option for him right now."

"Kyle?" Jason stops on the top step. "Alone with his thoughts in a cabin? I'm not so sure, Mitch."

"Why not? After what he went through here, it seemed like the change of scenery might do him good."

"Maybe. Maybe not." Jason looks behind him, down the empty beach. Other than the few tiki torches still lit, all evidence of the vow renewal fiasco is wiped clean. Chairs stacked, driftwood signs and flip-flop buckets stowed in Cliff's storage shed. "Think I'll take a quick ride and check up on him." As he says it, Jason turns and heads down the deck stairs to the sand.

"Jason, wait!" Carol is at the slider screen, calling from inside the cottage. "You should have a coffee first."

"No, Carol. I really don't have time." Another step down to the beach.

"But Jason ..."

From behind him, Jason hears that slider scrape open, then closed.

Carol's voice gets louder as she crosses the deck. "*Go, go, go.* You did so much tonight, taking care of Kyle. Even wading into the water and messing with your prosthesis. Back and forth here, to the beach cleaning up the decorations, to the storage shed. Calling Maris. Worrying *endlessly* about Kyle and his wife. And I saw you before, stacking the chairs." She waggles a stern finger at him.

"Saw what?" Mitch asks.

"His leg was bothering him, Dad. Enough that he had to sit and take a break." Carol walks to the top of the stairs and squints down at Jason. "You're *exhausted*, Mr. Barlow. So stay until you just catch your breath, for God's sake."

Mitch leans over from his seat to get a view of Jason on the stairs. "Give poor Kyle a few minutes to himself, too. Let him get his act together." Mitch shields his eyes against the darkness. "Hell, take ten minutes, my friend. Not even for Kyle." He pushes out another chair at the deck table. "But for *yourself*."

When Jason only silently deliberates, Carol does what she always does. She says it like it is, no holds barred. "You'll collapse otherwise. And we're having none of that. So I'll get you a coffee," she adds while turning to go back inside. "Piece of cheesecake, too."

And Jason knows. There's no arguing with these two. If nothing else, they're right. Dead right. He's running on fumes now. So he climbs the stairs and walks across the deck. It would probably help if he wasn't still in his best man suit. The pant legs are damp and sandy at the bottom from when he hauled Kyle out of the water earlier. His vest is unbuttoned, the white-rose boutonniere long gone—tossed out into the sea. His shirtsleeves have been cuffed and shoved up all night as he cleaned the beach. Yes, every bit of the pale gray suit is limp and wrinkled as he finally sits in that waiting chair.

"That's better," Mitch quietly says when Jason sits across from him.

It is. There's no denying it. Because what happens when Jason purely stops and takes a deep breath of salt air, is this: It hits him. Fatigue swings right around at him like a baseball bat hitting one out of the park. So in the night's shadows, he sits back, lifts his hands and lightly touches his fingertips to his closed eyes.

⁓

After opening the door, Elsa motions for Shane to go ahead into the old Foley's back room. Standing in the doorway, she takes in the details the same way he might. From the original creaking wood-planked floor, to the dusty pinball machine in the corner, to the refurbished restaurant booths and screen door to the deck, to even the dorm-sized fridge on the counter—it's all here. All intact.

Some time capsule from Shane Bradford's youth has been preserved, unearthed and opened before his very eyes. She can tell by his whispered *Holy shit* and his slow steps into the room.

"Jason wouldn't take on the renovation without a specific clause in our contract," Elsa says from behind Shane. "This room was to remain untouched. A museum to all you beach kids, I guess."

"Jason?" Shane turns to Elsa. "Jason Barlow? He's your architect?"

"Sure is."

Shane pays the highest compliment he probably can, given the circumstances of his uncomfortable presence here at Stony Point. He takes off his newsboy cap for a better look and gives a long, low whistle.

"It's something, isn't it?" Elsa sits in one of the booths. From what she could always tell by all the stories she's heard—by the *Remember whens* and *Back in the days*—this room is haunted. Tonight's the proof. In the dust particles swirling in the glowing jukebox light, Shane must hear echoes of some old summer song; might see misty ghosts spinning in a slow dance across the shadowy wood floor.

"It's crazy, Elsa. What a time warp." Shane runs his fingers across the glass dome of the jukebox, then walks to the pinball machine. "So many memories. I mean, I can just see the card games, the rowdy nights here. A few drinks, a few dances. The laughs. The arguments." He taps the pinball flippers, then turns and pulls a pair of drumsticks from a shelf. "Neil's?"

"They are. The originals, from back then. An extra pair we found during the reno."

Shane hits them in his open palm, twice. "Damn," he quietly says. "Back in the day, Neil would keep the beat to some jukebox song. He'd tap a table edge, or his own lap. I'd join in with my harmonica and we'd get everybody going."

"I can just picture that," Elsa says from her booth.

When he returns the drumsticks to the shelf, a framed photograph on the wall grabs Shane's attention. It's the picture of the whole gang taken last summer on the night of Maris' homecoming party, once she'd returned from a fashion trip to Europe. After celebrating here, everyone walked to the beach together. Someone built a small campfire and asked a passerby to take the shot as the friends all hung out together. Shane walks to the driftwood-framed picture, riveted, and stops directly in front of it.

"That was taken last year," Elsa explains. "Some familiar faces, I'm sure?"

"Wait." Shane touches the glass, then looks back at Elsa. "That's *Maris*."

"Yes, it is."

"What's she doing here?"

"She lives here. It was *her* wedding that brought me back to Stony Point. She's my family. My niece."

"You're kidding." He squints over at Elsa. "Now, wait. Her mother died when she was a child, so you're …"

"Her mother's sister."

"*Her mother's sister, her mother's sister,*" he whispers. "The one who gave her the star necklace?"

Elsa merely nods, rather taken aback by Shane's awareness of that cherished pendant, and so by *his* undeniable history here, too. Yet she'd never heard a mention of him from anyone.

Shane stuffs his cap into his back pocket and steps closer to the picture. It's as though he's starved for some story, for details of the lives he's seeing. "And Maris is married ... to *Jason*?"

Elsa looks past him at the picture. In it, Jason sits behind Maris on the sand and is kissing the side of her head. "For two years now."

Again Shane turns to Elsa. He gives a quick shake of his head. "What the hell's Maris doing living in this harbor town? I mean," he adds with another glance at the photo. "She's a fashion designer. Shouldn't she be living in New York? Or L.A.?"

A moment passes when Elsa only looks at him. "You really *have* been gone a long time. Much has changed." She leaves the booth and walks to the photo. It must be difficult to see all these familiar faces after not being in touch for fifteen years. How can you not help but wonder, but scrutinize, but search for some old connection.

To piece together the puzzle of all the days and lives since.

In the picture, Lauren kneels beside Kyle with her head on his shoulder; Maris is with Jason; Matt and Eva sit off to the side, leaning close; Sal watches Celia strum her guitar beside the fire.

"That's Maris, of course," Elsa whispers. The moment feels that serious. "And her sister, Eva."

"Wait. *Sisters?*"

"Oh, yes. Long, long story. And they were as surprised as you are now to learn that bit of information."

"My *God*. Sisters." He looks at the photo again, pointing this time to Jason's prosthetic left leg. "Jason. His leg's injured. Was he in the service?" When Elsa hesitates, he continues. "At war?"

"No, Shane. Jason lost his leg, from the knee down, in a terrible motorcycle accident."

"What? I can't believe all this." He looks at Elsa again. "I mean, I *do*. But it's almost unfathomable. In my mind, time stopped fifteen years ago—when I was last here."

"Oh, but time always marches on, Shane." She gives him a small smile. "Just like those tides of the sea that you love. They never stop rising and receding, just like the days."

He turns to the picture once more. Except now he lifts it right off the wall hook and studies it closely. A full red moon hangs low in the sky behind the friends. The campfire flames cast a soft glow on their faces. If Elsa had to say so, that one night, every one of them seemed happy. Or content. So *in* the moment, together.

"Neil wasn't here this night? Did he move away or something? Because, man, this was the type of night he *lived* for."

Elsa takes the framed picture from Shane. She runs her

own hand over the glass, then rehangs the photograph on the wall hook. "Neil," she whispers. "That motorcycle accident? When Jason lost his leg? His brother died in the same crash."

"Neil? Neil's *dead*?"

"Do you mean to tell me that no one *ever* told you?" Elsa tips her head in disbelief. "Not in all these years?"

"No." Shane looks around the dimly lit room—at the jukebox, and pinball machine, and booths beside the sliding windows—as though seeking Neil somewhere in the shadows. Finally his gaze returns to the photograph. "Neil's really *gone*?"

"I'm afraid so. Ten years now. I'm truly sorry you didn't know. Neil actually died a month before your brother and Lauren got married."

Elsa looks at the picture, too. Oh, ghosts are hovering close. They often do, in this room. But tonight? If she looks a certain way, can't she picture Neil somewhere on the outskirts of that photograph? Standing further down the night beach, his jeans cuffed, his thick hair lifting in a sea breeze? Though she never even knew him, Neil is somehow a presence in all their lives here, Shane's included.

"And of course, you met my assistant innkeeper, Celia, the other day," Elsa finally adds. She reaches around Shane's shoulder and points her out. "That's her—playing the guitar and sitting next to little Aria's father."

A ringing cell phone interrupts them then. Elsa hurries to where she left her phone in the booth and quickly takes the call, especially when she sees that it's Celia's father. He's babysitting Aria in the guest cottage.

"The baby's good?" she asks.

"Very good. No worries, Elsa. I'm just checking in. And I talked to Celia, too."

"She's still with Lauren?"

"Just left there. She mentioned that she had one stop to make on her way home. Something about flowers on a boat?"

"Oh, yes. Lauren was going to arrive at the ceremony in that rowboat. I'm sure Celia wants to get the wedding flowers off it now. I forgot all about it in the boat basin," Elsa tells him. "But that could've waited until morning I suppose," she adds with a worried glance out at the night. "Though the marina has some lights on, so she should be okay."

When Celia's father assures her that Celia said she wouldn't be long, and that Aria's asleep anyway, Elsa thanks him for watching the baby. "You have a good night's rest," she says before ending the call. "And we'll talk in the morning."

"I'm going to call it a night, too, Elsa," Shane says when she sets down her phone. He gives another look at the photograph hanging on the wall, then pulls on his newsboy cap, tugging it low. "Might sneak in that beach walk first, though. Before I turn in."

Elsa gets up and squeezes his hand. "It's a lot to take in, I know," she says with a nod to the wall photograph.

"I'll say." He gives a last look back at the picture. "I'm

tired, too. But a walk will do me good. Breathe some of that salt air at the end of one long day. Cures what ails you," he quietly adds.

So apparently the day's been difficult for Shane as well. Especially tonight. Watching him open the back room's creaking screen door and go down the deck stairs to the sandy beach road, his sudden departure says it all. It's like one of those mighty ocean waves suddenly turned in a breeze and washed over him just now, dousing him but good.

Difference is, this wave came *not* from a sea breeze, but from the past.

From that driftwood-framed photograph of the beach friends together a year ago, one misty summer night, beneath the light of the moon.

nine

11:30 p.m. – Saturday

THE FIRST THING JASON NOTICES on Sea View Road is the flashing lights of emergency vehicles. Especially with the way those lights sweep across neighboring cottages. Yellow and red, the spinning beams also fall on shadows of folks clustered together, pointing, standing near the edge of the bluff. Beneath the sporadic lights, the scene's almost nightmarish—well suited to Jason's own night.

One vehicle in particular gets his attention. It's Cliff's security car, parked all askew. Cliff left his headlights on, apparently to shine even more light on whatever catastrophe is going down over on the rocks. Parking alongside Cliff's car, Jason then makes his way through the crowd of vacationers watching some middle-of-the-night spectacle.

And a spectacle it is. A sailboat somehow got itself

marooned on the rocks. The vessel is leaning there, on its side. With the tide high, waves lap at its hull, over and over again. In the illumination of high-powered flashlights, as well as Cliff's headlights, the water shifts the turquoise-blue boat with each incoming splash.

"Commish, what happened?" Jason asks after traipsing down to the rocks.

"Oh, Jason," Cliff says while looking over his shoulder. "Surprised to see you."

"Couldn't miss all the commotion."

Cliff looks past Jason, then back at him. "Where's Kyle? You found him, right? I got the text."

"He's around. So I've only got a few minutes. What's going on here?"

"Beached boat, Barlow. Some kids were out horsing around on it. They all jumped in for a swim and the sailboat wasn't moored. Tide washed it up here."

"Damn." Jason draws his hand down his jaw and squints out at the damaged boat. "What a shame."

"Sure is. Might be a total loss."

"Did the boat belong to the kids' parents? Or was it stolen?"

"What?" Cliff tips up his COMMISSIONER cap and eyes Jason.

"Stolen, man." Oh, doesn't Jason remember the night they stole the old commissioner's boat back when they were teenagers. Took that sweet little cabin cruiser for a good joyride on the Fourth of July before getting caught. "Bored teens on a hot Saturday night, doing a little hot-wiring?"

"Well, now." Cliff pulls out a notepad and begins

jotting. "You might be onto something there."

"Yeah. Experience taught me well."

"Experience? You mean to say—"

"Never mind me." Jason leans forward for a better look at the crashed boat, then turns to Cliff. "So how'd it go at the inn? You get Shane out of there, no problem?"

"About that. Here's the thing …" Cliff drops his notepad back into his jacket pocket. "Now listen, Jason. And don't get mad."

"Mad?" Jason steps closer, watching Cliff.

"It's just that I've been waylaid and haven't gotten to the inn yet. Several problems cropped up tonight, including a gosh-darn raccoon trapped in a garbage can."

"Are you kidding me?"

"I'm not. But remember, it's the weekend." Cliff waves his arm to the beached sailboat. "And trouble always amps up here on weekends. You know that."

"No. What I *know* is that you were supposed to get to Elsa's inn, right away. And that was hours ago! The hell with all this," Jason insists, waving to the small crowd half-watching him and Cliff now. "Have one of your security guards handle things here."

"I *am* the commissioner of this beach. And my priority is folks' safety."

"Safety? From a scavenging raccoon?" Jason steps closer and lowers his voice. "Do you know how critical it is that Shane Bradford not be ensconced in some cozy coffee chat with Elsa? How imperative that he be booted off her premises?"

"I do."

"He's got to be ousted, Cliff." Jason pushes his sleeve back and checks the time on his watch. "Shit. I thought I could count on you, man."

"You can. The inn's next on my list."

Jason turns to leave, then turns back to Cliff and jabs his shoulder. Dropping his voice, he warns him. "*Don't* let me down, *Sailor*. It means *that* much."

"On second thought … Can't you do it?" Cliff asks as he motions onlookers away from the rocks. "Really got my hands full here. And you squared things away with Kyle—"

"No. Because I'm actually on my way out. And hell, we had a *deal*, Raines. You good for your word?"

"Yeah, yeah. I'm *on* it," Cliff relents, backing up a step. "I called the marina to reserve a crane and barge for the morning. It'll have to lift this vessel off the rocks if we can't summon the manpower to finagle it off." He looks over his shoulder and keeps walking back toward the boat wreck. "Just have to finish blocking off the area with safety cones and caution tape. And schedule another security guard to keep watch here tonight."

Throwing up his hands, Jason walks away, weaving through the small crowd gathered. "Excuse me," he says while squeezing past the families. "Excuse me, please." When he looks over his shoulder, there's Cliff caught in the light of his security cruiser's headlight beams. Cliff's got both arms outstretched now as he presses the onlookers further away from the scene.

Right then, one of the new guards gives Cliff a

megaphone, which he lifts to his mouth. *"Can I have your attention?"* Jason hears.

Which is enough.

Enough to know it'll be a God damn long time before Cliff untangles himself from this shipwreck and is able to finally evict Shane.

⁓

And Jason has more pressing matters to attend to. So he gets into his parked car and books it down Sea View, finally turning onto Bayside Road. He's got one destination and one destination only right now.

It's the Bradfords' bungalow by the bay. He can't miss it, with those tiny white lights twinkling around the windows. He parks in the driveway, knocks on the screen door, then opens it and walks right onto the porch.

"Lauren!"

"Jason?" Lauren rushes through the living room, turning on a tabletop lamp as she does. She's still wearing her frayed denim shorts with a loose black top. "What are you doing here? I thought you were with Kyle."

"I was." Jason steps through the doorway to the living room. "Listen, where are your kids?"

"At my parents' house. Why?"

"Okay, good. We're going somewhere, you and I. Quick, throw some things in an overnight bag. For Kyle, too. Then we'll lock up here."

"What? Overnight bag?" Her voice drops as she steps

closer. "Kyle's not in the hospital, is he? And don't you lie to me, Jason Barlow."

"No. No, Kyle's fine. I'll fill you in on the way. Hurry up, go pack," he insists, waving her off and turning back to the porch. "Wait!" he calls out when he sees a crumb-covered platter with one untouched sandwich on it. He picks up a neatly sliced half and lifts the top bread slice to find a chicken cutlet and cheese, all covered with fresh tomato and mayo. "Hang on a sec!"

"What now?" Lauren asks, flying onto the porch in a near panic. "What's the matter?"

"Nothing, it's just ... Do you mind?" Jason asks, holding up the sandwich. "I haven't eaten all day."

"Oh, *that*. Go ahead. It's from Eva. She made a whole tray of those."

"A tray?" Jason bites into the cooled, toasted sandwich. "You might want to pack a few of *these*, too," he says around a mouthful, then wipes a dribble of some magical dressing from his chin. "You know. For Kyle."

All Lauren does is raise an eyebrow when Jason manages to finish off the sandwich half in two big bites.

"I could really use another one, too," he admits after chewing and getting some of the best-sandwich-he's-ever-had swallowed.

"Okay. I better hurry, then," Lauren says while turning back inside. "There's a small cooler in the top cabinet in the kitchen, if you want to start wrapping sandwiches."

"I have to call Maris first," Jason shouts from the porch doorway.

Wiping a paper napkin across his mouth, he works on the second sandwich half. Jason's not sure he's ever had a better cutlet sandwich. Either that, or he's just so famished, anything would taste that sweet. As soon as Lauren runs upstairs to her bedroom, he first looks inside toward the kitchen, where the other sandwiches need wrapping. After finishing his own sandwich while standing in place, he hesitates, then walks outside to the front lawn before he just stops. The whole night's been an emotional tug of war like that: Push, pull. Hurry, wait. Back, forth. This way, that. Go, stop. Which he finally does.

Stops and hears the lapping waves of the bay across the street. It's too dark to see them, but it doesn't matter. The sound is enough. It gets him to take a breath, then another. The moon's risen higher in the sky, and that's all he sees. Far over the bay, silver moonlight shines on the calm water, the water Kyle calls his own now.

Jason pulls a flattened cigarette from his pocket—one Kyle had given him earlier. He lights it, takes a long drag, then pulls out his phone to call his wife.

At this hour, Celia's not sure which throws more light: that nearly full moon rising high over the Sound, or the few streetlamps around Stony Point's boat basin. In the still, dark water, fifty or so boats are docked. Small cabin cruisers, fishing skiffs and motorboats look like pale white ghosts beneath the night's misty illumination.

After parking the golf cart, Celia grabs the garden gloves and plastic garbage bags from the passenger seat. Removing that forgotten flower arrangement from the inn's rowboat is the least she can do for her devastated friend. So Celia unlatches the marina gate onto the concrete walkway circling the moored boats. A fine layer of sand is gritty beneath her sandaled feet as she makes her way to the old rowboat—which can't be missed with those white roses spilling from it.

While nearing the wooden boat, she spots a man walking across the boardwalk on the far side of the marina. He's headed for the shade pavilion, where twinkling lights had been strung for the vow renewal ceremony. If she's not mistaken, it's Kyle walking there. So she slows her step and squints through the dim light. He's tall, well built, and has a slow, easy stride. Celia almost calls out to him until she notices that familiar newsboy cap. Her heart sinks then, knowing it's not Kyle after all. It's his brother, Shane.

As she starts walking again, Celia tosses another look in his direction. Because part of her wants to confront Shane. To yell, *How could you show up here? It's been a difficult year for everyone, and now you've gone and ruined this day, too.* It's the only way she knows how to defend Lauren, her heartbroken beach friend—by getting mad at the man who unhinged the day.

But a part of Celia is also intrigued. After all, Lauren *did* invite this Shane fellow to her ceremony. And all because of Sal, apparently, and his strong belief in second chances. The invitation was Lauren's private way of extending an olive branch to her brother-in-law.

So Celia *could* just call out a friendly hello.

Instead, she keeps walking to the rowboat. All around her in the marina, the moored boats creak and groan against the pilings to which they're secured. *Boat talk*, Sal once told her on an evening beach walk. *They're speaking a secret language of the sea.*

It hits her then, how very deeply she still misses Sal. If he were here, he'd have talked sense into everybody on this crazy day.

"Why'd you have to go and die?" she whispers. "We all needed you today, Sal. You, of all people, could have fixed things. Could've made us find the good."

When she gets to the decorated rowboat and sees the large spray of flowers up close, it reminds her of the arrangement of flowers on Sal's coffin last summer. She could weep with that thought, being alone in the boat basin now.

At least, she *was* alone.

Alone, until Shane Bradford crossed the boardwalk beyond the marina on some late-night stroll. Maybe it's better this way, so that she's not isolated here in the darkness. It's probably good to have a familiar face nearby.

But when Celia looks back over her shoulder, Shane has left. The boardwalk stretches empty across the night beach.

ten

11:40 p.m. – Saturday

"OKAY, BABE," MARIS SOFTLY SAYS into her cell phone. "Love you, and keep me posted. I'll be at Eva's a bit longer."

When she sets the phone on Eva's teak deck table, all Maris hears is water. Seawater flows in the channels winding through the marsh beyond the deck. There's something so peaceful about that rippling sound, contrary to what the day's been. Yet everywhere around her—in sound, in sight—there's that sereneness now. Nautical red, blue and yellow buoys hang from the side of Eva's deck posts. Stars twinkle in the dark sky. And the marsh grasses, tall and sweeping in mid-August, whisper sweet nothings into the night.

Maris rubs her bare arms against the damp air, then sips from her wineglass. Tiny white lights strung around the patio umbrella's spokes cast a glow on the table. In a minute, Eva comes out through the kitchen slider. She's got a jacket in each hand.

"What did Jason say?" her sister asks, sitting across from Maris.

"Huh. You won't believe this. Apparently Kyle actually went to that cabin he and Lauren reserved for their honeymoon."

"*Kyle* did? I'm surprised."

"I was, too. But I guess he's been at the Fenwick cottage tonight, with Jason, too."

"You mean, Carol's cottage? Right on the beach?"

"Apparently. Mitch Fenwick saw them near the rocks and invited them in when he noticed Kyle was in a bad way. They gave Kyle something to eat, a few cups of coffee to calm down. And Mitch convinced Kyle that going to the cabin in the woods would be a good thing. Told him something about Thoreau spending time alone in a cabin in the woods, too."

"Oh, no. No, no, no. I mean, Thoreau's one thing. But Kyle?"

Maris nods. "Jason's thoughts exactly. So he left the Fenwicks' and picked up Lauren. He's bringing her to that cabin—Chickadee Shanty, I think it is—as we speak. Problem is, Kyle doesn't know it yet."

Eva sips her wine, then bites into a slice of raspberry Danish she'd warmed earlier in the microwave. "I sure hope Jason knows what he's doing."

"Me, too. And on top of everything, he's completely exhausted."

"I'll bet. He was so worried about finding Kyle, then cleaning up the beach. I had no idea they were right here at the Fenwicks' place, too."

"Me, neither. What a night. I told Jason to hurry back and get some rest." Maris wraps her arms around herself and gives a shiver against the night's chill.

"Oh! Here." Eva hands her a denim jacket that Maris gave *her* years ago. "Matt and Tay are watching the Yankees game in the living room. If you're cold, we can go inside?" Eva asks while putting on a windbreaker.

"No. It's nice out here after the day we've had. This is all I need." As Maris lifts the soft denim jacket, she looks at the embroidery across the back. A trail of gold stars are delicately stitched from one shoulder to the other. "We just can't get away from Shane today, no matter where we are."

Eva lifts the wine bottle and tops off their glasses. "What do you mean?"

"I mean, I was *with* Shane when I made this jacket for you," Maris explains as she slips her arms into the sleeves. "And I remember that day like it was yesterday."

That long-ago afternoon was pure summer ease at the harbor in New London. Maris sat at a picnic table right on the docks. The old table was dried out and splintery, just like the docks themselves. Salty and seaworn. Sometimes the guys would get off the boats, then sit and talk right there at the picnic table. They'd compare stories—who hauled in more lobsters; who got injured; how rough the seas were. Or else, there were a few old-timers who'd sit on the docks and repair fishnet, or coil rope. On a sunny day, they'd bring a sandwich and have lunch at the old table.

But Maris? She'd set out her work on that table. It was nice, because the harbor was so close to Stony Point, fifteen minutes away. So she'd drive over and sketch there—it was such a pretty spot with the boats in the water. Other times she'd sew, like she did the day she finished Eva's jacket. That afternoon was perfect, all sunshine and blue skies. She put on her straw cowboy hat, spread the denim on the table and ran her hand over the shooting stars she'd inked across the shoulders, then got to work stitching.

Well, waiting was more like it. Because embroidering was just a distraction that helped pass the hours of what she was really doing. She was waiting for one particular boat to come into port: Noah's, the lobsterman Shane worked with. So she kept one eye on her stitching, one eye on the channel, watching for that old lobster boat.

But sitting there in the warm sunshine and salt air that day, she got completely lost in her design work. She was twenty years old, on summer break from college. And her sewing was meticulous by then, as she stitched each star to curve and tip just so ... like shooting stars. Maris was so engrossed, she didn't even see Noah's boat return; didn't even hear Shane come up behind her. But he did, quietly, when he lifted off her hat and kissed the top of her head. He sat beside her then, and she gave him such a big hug, like she always did.

"Careful," Shane said, laughing. "I'm all wet and covered with fish bait." With that, he brushed flecks of silver fish scales off his shirt.

"I don't care," Maris told him, then stretched over and kissed his tired face.

Night Beach

"*Your father know you're here?*"

She shook her head. "He thinks I'm at the beach. At Eva's."

Shane blew out a long breath, then ran his hand back through his salty hair. "What have you got there?" he asked, nodding to her denim jacket.

Maris lifted it and showed him the constellation of pale yellow stars taking shape. "I'm making this for Eva. A surprise, special for her, now that she's pregnant and going to be a mom."

"She'll like that."

"Hope so. Maybe it can be her something blue, for her and Matt's beach wedding. I could just see Eva wearing this over her shoulders, with her gown and all. Later on, to ward off the sea damp."

Shane lightly touched an embroidered star, giving a low whistle at the same time. "Really nice, Mare. You could sell jackets like this at the Stony Point craft fair. Make some serious cash off them."

"Maybe."

Then? An easy afternoon unfolded. Shane leaned his elbows back on the tabletop, stretched out his legs and tipped his face to the sun. He had on faded jeans, an old button-down over a tee. Beside him, Maris kept sewing, pushing her needle in and out of the denim. Tugging and pulling that thread to shape the last stars.

And it was nice, just the sound of their quiet voices, seagulls crying, and the creak of the run-down dock and the boats moored there. That day, Maris had packed a tote with sandwiches, and fruit and munchies. They ate and laughed there, too. Talked to some of the other lobstermen.

Ended up staying out on the dock so long, she actually finished stitching those intricate stars on the jacket. It's why she loved waiting for Shane at that picnic table, and doing some sketching or stitching.

She did her best work knowing he was headed back to her.

"What do you want to do now?" Shane asked when Maris was done embroidering.

She felt him touch the skin on her arm while waiting for her answer. Touch her arm, touch her hair twisted into a loose French braid. His fingers moved softly over her.

"Nothing," she whispered back.

And that's what they did. Nothing. Just sat there at the docks and listened to the water slapping at the moored boats. Heard the bell buoy clang further out in the channel. Breathed the salt air, watched the sun set.

As Maris tells her sister a little about that day at the New London docks, she holds back many of the details. Because the harbor memory brings every bit of those sweet hours back to her. Every sensation comes to life … the scent of the sea … the feel of Shane's touch … the sound of his voice.

"That was the beautiful thing," Maris instead says now, lightly twisting a strand of her own hair.

"What was?" Eva asks.

Maris looks at her and tips her head with a small smile. "So often those days, doing nothing with Shane … was everything."

eleven

11:45 p.m. – Saturday

THE TIDE IS HIGH, AND salt water slaps against the boats in the little Stony Point marina. Celia sits on the edge of the concrete walkway, stopped cold at the sight of the wooden rowboat loaded with flowers. Elsa wasn't kidding when she said the florist decorated it with an elaborate wedding arrangement. Around the bow, white roses shimmer beneath the moonlight. Delicate vines are draped over the boat's sides, the green tendrils skimming the rippling water. More than anything now, the enchanted sight is such a sad reminder of so many dashed hopes.

Lauren had given her a flashlight, and Celia shines it in front of her. The rowboat's pulling on its mooring and not close enough to step into. Even if she stretches and takes one leaping step, it's more likely she'll miss by inches and fall—silver dress and all—right into that deep, black water. So when she stands, she bends close and first tosses her garden gloves aboard the vessel. Then she grabs hold of the dockline rope and pulls the boat close enough to *somewhat* easily board.

Which she does, flashlight in hand. Her balance wavers as her foot hits the boat, and she quickly gets in, tips way to one side—arms outstretched—then promptly drops onto a bench.

"*Okay*," she whispers after taking a sharp breath. "*Made it.*" Another quick breath slows her pounding heart, and a look around helps to get her bearings. Only a few streetlight-type lamps illuminate the boat basin, just enough to light the concrete walkway circling the docked boats. Beyond the marina, except for those twinkle lights beneath the roofed shade pavilion, the boardwalk is a black silhouette against the night sky. To the west, a few cottages are mere shadows rising in the darkness out past the marina.

Still, Celia's shaken with visions of almost missing her step and plunging straight into the murky, saltwater depths. Shaken enough to barely peer over the edge of the boat, down into that cold, dark water lapping at the hull.

But she made it safely, even while wearing the fitted maid-of-honor dress she never had a chance to change out of. One thing's for sure: The quicker she gets started, the quicker she'll get out of here, back to the comfort of her own guest-cottage home behind the inn. So she stretches for a garbage bag—still on the concrete walkway where she'd dropped them before getting on the boat. Of course, they're just out of reach, so she tugs on that dockline to move the boat closer, half stands and leans forward to scarcely snatch up a bag.

"Got it," she says, sitting promptly again so as not to take that dunk overboard. After putting on her gloves, she directs the flashlight beam on the rose arrangement and starts pulling long stems off the boat's bow. When she gathers a big enough handful, she turns and stuffs it into the black garbage bag.

"It's a darn shame Lauren didn't get to have that rowboat ride for her vow renewal," a man says from the walkway.

Celia quickly looks over her shoulder at the surprising voice. It's Shane, standing two boats away. He's leaning against a dock post, watching her from beneath the brim of that newsboy cap of his.

"Oh, Shane. You've been there this whole …" Celia glances to where she'd last seen him on the boardwalk, then brushes back a strand of hair with her gloved hand. "Well. It was such a painful situation today for poor Lauren. Who happens to be a good friend of mine, so I'm doing her a favor." In a quiet pause, she leans forward from her bench seat and yanks another handful of roses, then stops and looks up at Shane still standing there, still watching her. But it's hard to read him behind the shadows on his face. "Why *are* you still here anyway? Surely you're aware that Kyle and Lauren's ceremony was cancelled, so you can leave now."

"Ceremony or not, I do have a beach weekend booked at the Ocean Star Inn."

"You're staying on? I don't get it." The rowboat pulls

against its dockline, the boat shifting in its slip. "Why would you even *want* to be here now? After all this," she says, sweeping an arm toward the sad flowers.

"In case somebody wants to talk to me. Lauren. My brother."

"That's doubtful," Celia quietly answers.

After watching her a few seconds longer, Shane picks up an empty garbage bag and easily steps into the rowboat. That much Celia notices—his sureness of step. There's no wavering balance, no outstretched hand searching for something to grab onto so as not to fall overboard. Just a smooth, light step before he stands steady in the now-rocking boat. Stands right in her way.

"Hey." She looks up at him. "What are you doing?"

"Let me help," he says. "You're Celia, right?"

"I am." She eyes him cautiously while holding the handful of roses she'd just pulled. "And the last thing *anybody* here wants is me talking to you tonight."

Shane reaches down and carefully removes an armful of the flower arrangement. When he straightens, the long vines drip salt water onto his jeans and his leather boat shoes. "You always do what other people want?" he asks.

"No." She opens the garbage bag for him. "Well, yes. Well, it *depends*! And you don't?" she asks as he drops his armful of flowers into the bag.

"Don't what?" he asks back.

"You don't do what people want? People you care about."

Shane sits beside her on the bench. His arms rest on his

knees as he cuffs the damp sleeves of a loose button-down he wears, first. That done, he looks her straight on. "I came to the vow renewal, didn't I? Like Lauren—who I care about—wanted me to."

"That's diff— Oh, never mind."

Because let's face it. He got her. Trapped her with her own words. So Celia instead warily removes more flowers from the boat's bow, then sets them in the bag Shane holds open for her. What she notices as she lowers her armful of rose blossoms are the tattoos covering both his forearms. In the dim lighting, she can't make them out, but sees the swirls and waves of ink beneath his folded shirt cuffs. Each tattoo, she's sure, has some rowdy story behind it.

But she says nothing and just tries to finish up this task so that she can get herself home. She keeps lifting bunches of rose stems and dripping vines, feels them snap beneath her gloved hands when she folds them to fit into the bag, then turns to the bow for more.

And that's how it goes. After the first bag's filled, they work on the second. The boat rocks with their efforts; seawater drips from the lifted vines; the scent of roses mixes with the pungent salt air. It's not an easy job, what with the thorns and fallen petals dropping in the boat. But together, the two of them remove the stunning floral array that held such promise for the day. The arrangement's dismantled an armful at a time, long stems at a time, both of them reaching, tugging and lifting the flowers and dripping vines from the bow of the boat.

When she and Shane both reach for the second garbage

bag opened at their feet, their hands brush.

"Close quarters here," Shane quietly says as he shifts out of her way. "Just like on the lobster boats."

"That's right. Lauren mentioned you're a lobsterman." As she tells him this, Celia puts the very last of the flowers into the garbage bag.

"That I am."

He says nothing more. He just stands, takes the stuffed bag, ties it up in a knot and steps easily out of the boat onto the walkway. There, he sets the bag with the other one already filled and tossed aside.

"Well ..." Celia begins as she grips the edge of the boat and slowly rises on unsteady feet. "That should do it. Thank you for your help." Glad to finally be on her way, she reaches her other hand for the flashlight on the bench.

"Whoa, whoa," Shane interrupts. "Hold up there."

Celia straightens, awkwardly shifting her feet to keep her balance in the rocking boat as she watches him closely.

"I still have my complimentary rowboat ride voucher from the Ocean Star Inn. And you know something? I'd like to cash it in tonight." With that, Shane tips his hat, then steps back into the little wooden boat. "Come on. You sit, I'll row."

twelve

11:50 p.m. – Saturday

"YOU'RE NOT TAKING THE HIGHWAY?" Lauren asks.

"Not yet," Jason says. "For now, the back roads are good. They're better for thinking."

"I'm afraid to think."

Jason glances over at Lauren sitting in his SUV's passenger seat. Her overnight bags and small cooler are tossed in the backseat; she wears a zip sweatshirt over her black lace-up top; her hair is still falling from that chignon. There'd been no time to fuss.

"Seriously, Jason. I'm also afraid it's a mistake for me to go to Kyle. He would've called me if he wanted me there."

"At this point," Jason tells her while driving the winding road, "Kyle doesn't know what he wants."

They're quiet then as the headlights shine on the dark pavement. This late at night, the beach roads look like ghost towns. Miles pass of moonlit marshes and lagoons, of empty bait shacks and ice-cream stands—all of it desolate now.

All of it gradually giving way to cornfields and farmhouses and white split-rail fences. Beach to rural, the strongest evidence is the air. When Jason takes a long breath, the saltiness is gone.

"I can't be alone with him. Kyle hates me right now." Lauren shifts in her seat to face Jason. "So if it turns bad in that cabin, what'll I do?"

"I'll talk to him first to feel him out."

"What will I even say to him, alone there?"

"Don't say much. Just get through this night together. Then get through tomorrow together. And the next day, and the next."

Does she hear it? That Jason speaks from experience? Does Lauren hear the times *he* had to get through a night, then one excruciating day at a time afterward?

When he regained consciousness after the motorcycle wreck a decade ago and discovered his brother was dead.

When he looked down in his hospital bed and saw how the wrapped bandages abruptly ended below his left knee.

When he relearned how to walk with a prosthetic limb. Then another when the first was a bad fit.

When he gave up the pain meds in the years following that wreck.

When his own wedding hung in the balance the night before he married Maris two summers ago.

Jason's *gotten through* a night too many times to count.

And now? Now it's Lauren's turn.

"Hike the trails at this lake Kyle talked about," Jason says while taking a wide curve on the country lane. "Go swimming. This is not the end of your marriage. It's a night. So … get through it."

"But I *really* hurt him."

"Lauren." He glances across the front seat at her. "If Kyle didn't *love* you, it wouldn't have hurt. No?"

Lauren stares at him for a second, then turns away and looks out the passenger window.

Outside now there is nothing but dark wooded areas with colonial homes set back from the road, here and there. They pass through a tiny town that holds not much more than a general store, car dealership and empty fairgrounds used a few weekends a year.

"Would you mind grabbing me another of those chicken sandwiches?" Jason asks. "I'm starving."

"Sure." Lauren reaches around to the backseat for her insulated tote. "Your dinner?" she asks while pulling out a sandwich and getting it unwrapped for him.

"More like a snack," Jason tells her when he takes the sandwich with one hand, the other on the wheel.

"Do you want to pull over to eat? I don't mind."

"Nah. Better to just keep going. Get to that cabin right away."

"Well, here's something to drink, too. And a napkin." She sets a water bottle and napkin in the console's cup holder. "Maris will probably have some leftover dinner for you when you get home."

"Maybe." Jason lifts the specialty cutlet sandwich, this one on a soft roll, and digs in while driving.

"Do *you* think I was wrong?" Lauren asks a long minute later. Her voice is almost a surprise in the now-quiet vehicle. "To invite Shane?"

"At first?" Jason answers around a mouthful of chicken and sweet native tomato slices. "I did. But as the day went on, maybe not. I could see what swayed you, thinking of second chances. I mean, how many chances do any of us have before it's too late? Lord knows I've had my share of second chances." He grabs another bite of the sandwich. "Had some third and fourth chances, too. But, you know. Do we have a quota of those God-given chances? Because what I wouldn't have given to talk to my brother Neil again. But I never had *that* chance."

Lauren reaches over and squeezes Jason's arm. "I know," she whispers. "Me, too."

Jason nods, then turns onto the entrance ramp to finally pick up the highway.

"I feel like I can't even talk to Kyle," Lauren says once they're on the interstate. "Everything was so good with us, and then I pulled this. What do I even say? I'm *sorry*?"

"Are you?"

"What?"

"Are you sorry that you invited Shane? Or are you sorry that it didn't work out the way you'd hoped?"

"Maybe." She cracks her window open and a stream of cool air fills the vehicle. "But you don't understand, Jason. Kyle and I've had too many hard knocks, starting way back with my affair with Neil. Then three years ago, we were out of money. Strapped. That was when the steel jobs dried up, so Kyle worked part-time at the diner. Just to get by, I started temping, too, *and* looking at duplexes for me and the kids."

Jason holds up his half-eaten sandwich, motioning for her to wait while he finishes chewing. "You were going to leave him?" he finally manages.

"I came very close."

Jason raises an eyebrow. "Wasn't aware of that."

"It was that summer when we first rented a cottage at Stony Point. We both felt like we were living with a stranger that year. So that *vacation*," she says, air-quoting the word, "was really a trial separation. Me at the beach for a few weeks, Kyle at home. And our marriage *barely* survived. Then the next summer, when you and Maris got married? Kyle found out Evan wasn't even his son, but was Neil's." She shakes her head and is quiet for a moment. "And now this Shane thing. How many times am I going to break that man's heart?" she whispers.

Jason checks his rearview mirror, then passes a slow-moving car. "Listen," he says. "Kyle's a big guy, with a *big* heart. Tough as nails, too. All those years ago when he was a union steelworker, building ships at the shipyards? He was badass, Lauren, seriously paying his dues back then. And he's always reacted hard—when push comes to shove. Hotheaded, you know? I guess sometimes you still get a glimpse of that."

"Like today. Oh, if you could've seen how upset he was when he confronted me."

"I saw enough, believe me. Don't forget, I'm Kyle's best man, too," Jason reminds her as he picks up what's left of his chicken-cutlet snack. "Kyle was mine, and I'm his. We've got each other's backs, so I'm *not* about to let this day take you two down," he assures her, all while folding the last of that sublime sandwich into his mouth.

"I'm not sure you can stop it."

"But it's always been *you*, Lauren. That guy's had his heart set on no one else. Ever since we stole old Commissioner Lipkin's boat twenty years ago when we were teenagers." Keeping one hand on the steering wheel, Jason washes down the last of his sandwich with a swig of the bottled water. "So if you and Kyle can survive twenty years, you can survive one day."

"I remember that night like it was yesterday, stealing that boat. Being out on the dark water and feeling the waves all choppy. It was a black sky that night, and a black sea, and I couldn't tell the difference between the two." With a long sigh, Lauren leans against the headrest. "We were all *kids*, though. What the hell did we even know then?"

"Maybe everything we needed."

And there it is. The truth of it. Having a few laughs, a few drinks. Lighting bottle rockets out on the Sound. Hanging out and hooking up. Living in the moment, not overthinking things, letting your heart—rather than your head—guide you. Sometimes it's enough.

As highway signs for the town of Addison come into view, Jason gives Lauren the plan. He takes the next exit, drives through Addison and finds the rutted one-lane entrance leading to the country cabin Kyle rented. The SUV shifts from side to side over heaves in the packed dirt road. Tall trees rise around them, the moonlight casting eerie shadows beneath them as though the forest is straight out of a foreboding fairy tale.

"I'll go in first and talk to him," Jason explains while driving slowly and grabbing his napkin to wipe his mouth. "You wait for me here, and I'll do the best I can. Then I'm leaving."

"Right away? But what if things go bad? What if I have to leave, too?"

"You can call me. Anytime." Jason maneuvers the vehicle into a small parking area. "I'll come back and pick you up, if you need me to." He stops within view of the rustic cabins set around a tiny lake. "But I'm not waiting here. It'd be too easy of an out for both of you."

"I get it. I don't like it, but I get it."

Jason checks out the small cabins. Some are painted; one's an A-frame. Most are tiny wood-framed bungalows with front porches, lamplight spilling from the windows. Each lakeside dwelling is nestled among the trees. "Which cabin's yours, anyway?"

"It's that one," Lauren says, pointing out her window. "Chickadee Shanty. God, Jason. This was supposed to be our fun little getaway. You know, where me and Kyle's vow of celibacy was going to get tossed to the wind."

"Maybe it still will be, Lauren." Jason leans forward and gives a look. Chickadee Shanty is a peaked, white-painted cabin with a dark brown front door. Lamplight fills the paned windows, so Kyle must be inside. Two rocking chairs are on the open front porch. Cozy as can be, you'd think.

But you'd think that only if you hadn't come off a day that just turned *all* your thoughts upside down. A day that pulled the rug out from under you and left you reeling.

A day that made the looks of *everything* seem deceptive— that little cabin, included.

"Are you sure about this? Us going in there?" Lauren asks.

"No. Not really." Jason throws another glance at that cabin where Kyle's hiding himself away. "But my father used to give me and Neil advice when we were afraid of something. Or if we felt unsure." Jason takes one deep breath, thinking of his father's words. "Sometimes in 'Nam, he'd say, when they didn't know what they were dealing with, didn't know how to get through the jungle and enemy territory ... When his platoon was scared shitless? They'd just have to tell themselves that they *did* know how to do it."

When Lauren looks at him, desperate for more, for help, he only gives her a regretful smile. Putting the SUV in gear again, he slowly drives closer and parks beside Kyle's pickup at the edge of the small lot. From there, a winding stone footpath leads to the distant cabins.

Jason gets out, brushes sandwich crumbs off his gray suit pants, then leans back inside the open door and looks his devastated beach friend straight on. "So *tell* yourself you know what to do, Lauren, and you might be surprised to find that you damn well do."

thirteen

Midnight

THE SOUND LULLS CELIA. IT'S like some kind of tonic on this crazy night, that *drip-drip-dripping* whenever Shane lifts the oars and pauses for a moment. Then he sets the wooden oars in the water and slowly pulls back on them again, moving the rowboat further out the channel to Long Island Sound.

But that *drip-drip* of seawater off the oars does it. It gets Celia to loosen her tightly crossed arms. Gets her shoulders to drop. Gets her to take a longer breath as she sits there in her silver dress, her legs folded beneath the bench seat. When she reaches to dip her fingers into the seawater, her sandaled foot knocks over a bucket.

"Oh, shoot," Celia says, leaning down and scooping up spilled seashells and pieces of sea glass.

"Collecting those for your daughter?" Shane asks.

"No." She glances at him, then continues scooping. "My

father's the sea glass collector. He's always on the hunt for it."

"Really ..."

She nods, tucking a loose strand of hair behind her ear. "What he likes about it is the way the sea glass tells the story of passing time." She picks up a few pieces from the boat bottom and holds them up to the moonlight. "The glass, it's all worn smooth. And by what? Years and years of time in the sea."

Shane simply paddles, not saying anything. Just watching her while listening. The water laps at the boat's sides as he gets them out deeper.

"So," Celia continues after an awkward pause, "when I told Lauren that story, she liked the idea for her vow renewal. Because she said her marriage to Kyle is worn smooth now, and the rough edges are gone. So she wanted to scatter seashells and sea glass while they said their vows." Celia drops a few periwinkles and speckled slipper shells into the pail.

"Lauren thought of everything."

Then? Nothing. Just that *drip-dripping* from the oars as Shane listens to her story.

As, okay, this tough lobsterman listens to her little sea glass tale.

"Anyway, this day was important for Lauren. And now everything's ruined," Celia says with a sad smile. "Toppled just like this bucket." She picks up the last few pieces of sea glass and a couple of blue mussel shells. All the while, she's fully aware of Shane's slow and deliberate rowing. "I'm still not sure this is a good idea, this boat ride," Celia finally admits.

"I'd just like to see the beach from here." He keeps paddling, the oars rippling through the calm water as they head further out. "It's a nice view from a boat, and I haven't had a good look at this place in ages."

"We won't be too long?" she asks.

When Shane shakes his head, Celia tucks the bucket of shells and sea glass beneath the bench. The air's damp on the water, so she tightens Lauren's cardigan over her silver dress. As the rowboat rounds the bend out of the channel and approaches the big rock, the beach comes into her sights.

"It *is* really pretty from here." Celia says, glancing at Shane sitting on the other bench. "You're right."

When he nods toward shore, Celia wraps her arms around herself and takes in the shadowy view. The crescent-moon-shaped beach is nestled into the coast. At the far end, the patch of woods is a dark silhouette hugging the rocky outcropping where the guys like to fish. But the beach itself looks like a faded watercolor painting beneath the light of the nearly full moon. The sand is barely golden at nightfall, the water a liquid slate—both awash in pale moonbeams. Lamplight from the last-standing cottage on the beach spills from its windows and reflects off Long Island Sound directly in front of it. The entire seascape is cloaked beneath a velvet black sky dappled with stars.

As she twists around on the bench for a better look, she realizes how quiet Shane has gotten. *Well of course*, she thinks. *This magical view will do that.* There's the boardwalk shade pavilion still strung with twinkling lights for the cancelled vow renewal, and that misty moon—all of it glimmering on the night beach. But when she slightly turns to steal a glimpse at him behind her, Shane's looking only at her.

"I don't remember you," he says.

"What?" Celia sits up straight and turns toward him.

He pulls on the paddles, and the oars creak against the oarlocks. "From back in the day."

"You wouldn't remember me. I only arrived here last summer."

"But you're very familiar with everyone?"

"I didn't want to be, though." Celia looks toward that one stretch of beach where her whole life changed last summer. Her voice is faraway and she doesn't look at Shane as she explains. "I came here to lick some personal wounds and instead got sucked right into the lives here. Sucked into this *world*," she says with a nod to the deceptively tranquil beach, "that is Stony Point."

"So not by choice?"

"Not at first. But then?" She barely smiles, mostly to herself. "The summer days last year? They worked like time on sea glass, and softened all the rough edges of my life." Holding her sweater closed, she still stares out at the beach. "But not right away. Those first few weeks here? I had every doubt in the book. Oh, I wanted to hightail it out of Stony Point so many times."

Behind her, again there's only silence. Whether Shane's

watching her or the beach, it doesn't much matter right now. Because she's only interested in seeing the vague memories, the spirits on the beach from this vantage point. *Seeing* the times she walked the beach with Sal; *seeing* the clamshell toss at the Summer Shindig on their first date; the nights he danced with her at the water's edge; the campfire where she strummed her guitar as all the friends gathered 'round.

"Doubts about being here? Totally get that," Shane finally says. "I never would've come back to Stony Point now, not of my own accord. I'm only here because Lauren put out the invite. Wasn't sure why she did, so I pretty much thought it could be only one thing. Maybe my brother was sick or something, and I should see him."

Celia turns to face him. "No, it wasn't like that. Kyle's fine."

"What was it then? What moved my sister-in-law to reach out?"

"Oh, it's a complicated story, Shane. And not mine to tell. Except to say that Lauren and Kyle planned one heck of a celebration after a rocky first ten years of marriage."

Shane looks out at the distant beach as their rowboat drifts, the water lapping at its sides. "Life's been that bad for those two?" he asks.

"You'd have to talk to *them*." Celia zips her fingers across her lips. "Not my story to tell."

"So it sounds like they've had their share of dirty days."

"What do you mean?"

"Dirty days." He rests the oars on the boat and eyes her

from beneath that newsboy cap. "It's what me and the boys call a rough day at sea. Foggy, just dripping cold. Monster waves crashing over the deck. Days when you can barely stand straight without going overboard. Can hardly get the traps baited. You're drenched through, dirty in the slop and slimy bait all over the heaving boat." Again, he lifts the oars and gives a paddle. "A dirty day. They're tough to get through. Especially out on the open sea."

Celia watches him in the darkness. "So what drew you to it, then? To being out there like that all the time?"

"At first?" Shane sets the paddles in the boat and drops anchor, right there beyond the big rock. "A goddamn big chip on my shoulder. Me and Kyle were both raised by only our father after our mom got sick. And I didn't make things easy for Dad. I was a punk teenager, in and out of trouble. Saw the inside of a few courtrooms, had a few run-ins with the law. Until a community service stint got me on my first lobster boat, which was actually the perfect place for me— a kid with anger issues who'd been drinking and fighting as a result. Shoving off from the docks at three-thirty in the morning was a damn good wake-up call, for starters."

"So lobstering gave you a purpose."

"More like a challenge. I needed to face the biggest, baddest thing possible just to figure things out. And to put me in my place."

"Did it work?"

He shrugs. "Over the years, the sea wore that chip right down—just like your sea glass. Now? Now I can't wait to get on the dock and throw my bags onto the boat. No better sound than hearing that duffel hit the deck when I start each trip. It's where I spend my days. Gulf of Maine, mostly. On the sea," he says, nodding out toward the Sound behind them. "Cruising it, fighting it, hauling traps, getting through storms and the nasty temperament the waters can spit at you." He pauses then, and surprisingly tips his cap at her. "I'm not the same person I was fifteen years ago, thanks to the Atlantic Ocean."

Celia looks at him, then turns toward the distant beach. She wraps her arms around herself again and just feels the rise and fall of the sea beneath her. Murky water slaps against the sides of the anchored rowboat.

From what Celia's heard from everyone here, Shane's a problem. He's bad news ... nothing but trouble. The headstrong younger brother who, through his sheer presence alone, broke down Kyle today.

But after talking with Shane, she's not seeing all that. He speaks with thought. Listens closely. Sure, she *could* believe him—that a challenging life at sea softened his hard edges.

Either it did, or else Shane Bradford's a damn good liar.

fourteen

12:30 a.m. – Sunday

OKAY, SO JASON *ALMOST* TUGS the rat-a-tatting woodpecker doorknocker's pull-string. But he doesn't. Standing there on the dark porch, instead his knuckles give a sharp rap on Chickadee Shanty's painted-wood door.

"Jason," Kyle says when he opens that door. Kyle's still in his wrinkled cargo shorts and tee; circles shadow his eyes; he needs a shave. "You didn't have to come all the way out here. I'm fine now."

"Wrong." Jason steps past him and walks inside. "I *had* to make the trip. I'm your best man, dude."

"Doesn't mean you run my life. Remind me to pick Vinny for my best man next time," Kyle says when he closes the door.

"So you're saying there *will* be another vow renewal?"

"Jesus, Barlow." Kyle turns to Jason waiting for his answer. "Hey, you look like shit," Kyle tells him instead.

"Still in those suit pants? Got all dressed up, and for what?" he asks, walking past him to a planked farm-style table with a pinecone basket centerpiece.

Which gets Jason to look around at this little cabin. An antler coatrack hangs near the door; a burlap ribbon is entwined through a twig wreath beside the paned front window; a large birch branchlet hangs over the stone fireplace; knitted throws and hooked pillows cover the matching plaid sofa and overstuffed chair.

"It's not too late, you know," Jason says when he picks up, then sets down, one of many carved wooden chickadees scattered on end tables.

"Too late for what?"

"To renew your vows. I'm sure Elsa would still officiate. Even if it's tomorrow sometime."

Kyle looks at him, then paces the small living room. He nearly trips on a white birch-bark-wrapped tin stuffed with lavender stems beside the hearth. He's sweating, too. Perspiration beads on the side of his face.

"All right, man. Forget it," Jason says. "You don't have to do the vow renewal thing. Fine. But take a few breaths, would you? You're looking pale."

Kyle drags a finger around his tee collar and does just that, taking one long breath, then another, before sitting in that red-and-cream plaid stuffed chair. "Okay," he says while leaning back with a sigh. "Okay. I feel better now."

"Perfect." Jason sits on the sofa across from him and leans his elbows on his knees. "Then it's a good time for me to tell you that your wife's here."

"What?"

"And *I'm* leaving."

Which he is. Jason's about had it. Not so much with Kyle, but with the day—one now stretching into two days. Even though he sat with a hot coffee at the Fenwicks' before coming here, he's beat; his leg aches; his clothes are ruined. All Jason wants to do is get home, where he can crash for the next twenty or so hours before Monday cranks up a new week. So when Kyle starts in with him now, he's seriously testing Jason's threadbare patience.

"Lauren's *here?*" Kyle stands and walks to the paned window beside the door. "I've got nothing to say to her. I mean, not *yet*, anyway. I have to *think*, first, which is why I came out to the cabin, don't you get it? To pull my head together. Because, hell. Only yesterday, I thought I'd have this epic ten-year anniversary vow renewal and change the course of the *next* ten years. Make them great, you know?" He looks back to Jason, then out the window again. "But my wedding was a nightmare a decade ago, and it was a nightmare this weekend. So I don't know. Can't change history, can't change jack *shit*."

Okay, Kyle went and did it. He sapped any last thread of Jason's patience. So Jason lifts his weary bones off the sofa and walks over to where Kyle squints out toward the parking area. "You're an ass," Jason says. When he gets to the window, he gives Kyle a slight shove. "And you need to fucking calm *down*."

Kyle, all six-feet-two of him, eyes Jason for only a second before shoving him right back.

Well, that's it. Jason has his answer.

After hours of searching for Kyle; and worrying about him; and talking him through things; and coffeeing him up at the Fenwicks'; and ordering Cliff to get Shane out of the inn; and clearing out the white chairs from the beach; and bringing Kyle's wife to him here at the cabin, that answer comes loud and clear. *Nothing* will get through to Kyle today.

Not after his long-estranged brother, Shane, dropped hook, line and sinker—straight into Kyle's life.

No. When push comes to shove, which it just did, Kyle is about to lose everything. Everything he has, everything he loves. Panicked, he's about to bring to ruin everything around him. Himself, his family, friends. His marriage.

So Jason grabs him by the shirt collar and slams him into the wall, hard. "Can't change jack shit?" Jason repeats. "So, what then? Is this what you want instead? A divorce from Ell?" Jason drops his voice. "You never want to tell Lauren again that you love her? Never live with her and the kids in your house by the bay?" Jason looks away and takes a breath, then shoves his arm across Kyle's chest. "Because you know something, Bradford? You still *have* all that, asshole. So don't fuck up and lose it. You lose it, it's *gone*." Still holding Kyle against the wall, Jason continues. "Is that what you want, Kyle? Is it?"

Kyle makes a move then. He tries to push Jason away.

"Wrong answer," Jason tells him, his arm still locking Kyle against that wall. "Because when something's gone— Lauren, your family—it's gone. There's no getting it back.

And I'm living proof," he harshly whispers, inches away from Kyle's face. "Take a *good* look at me." As he says it, Jason feels his own perspiration; his haggard eyes and shadowed face; his tired clothes. "My leg, my mobility. Never coming back. And my brother?"

Kyle looks away, wordlessly. Because he damn well knows the answer to that one.

"I'm about to watch you screw up and lose everybody, and why? Because of some *ridiculous* pact we all made around a bonfire when we were young and stupid?"

Finally Kyle breaks out of Jason's armlock. "Fuck off."

"You want to be stubborn and obstinate? Take what you have for granted?" Jason lowers his voice. "You want to lose it all?" He puts every *shred* of his impatient rage into a sharp flick of his fingers at Kyle's chest. "Do it, man." With that, Jason turns and swings the little cabin's door open to the black night. "Do it. Walk out on everything you love. Your wife, your kids and house. Your marriage, for Christ's sake. All because Lauren sent out one God damn invitation to your brother."

When he stops, Jason realizes something that he didn't before—it's his own chest heaving to catch a breath. So he does, taking one long inhale before telling off the groom. "*Do* it. Get the hell out and keep on walking."

~

Some things you never see coming. Oh, doesn't Celia know it. Take Aria, for instance. Her precious daughter, an unexpected and beloved gift in her life. And there was Sal, breezing in and out of her days like a rogue wave, gone forever now. Even her job as an assistant innkeeper here on the Connecticut coast, and her home in a fairy-tale guest cottage. The shiniest crystal ball could never have revealed her beach life in its glass.

And now this. How could Celia have ever seen where this day would ultimately take her—anchored at sea.

Well, anchored in Long Island Sound near the big rock, anyway, Stony Point Beach misty in the moonlight just onshore. Every now and then, a school of minnows swishes the surface of the salt water. The noise is soft, bubbling, as some mean blue is on the hunt behind them.

"I have to get back, Shane." Celia glances overboard, then squints to check her watch. It's well after midnight. "My father's watching my daughter, and I need to be home now."

Shane gives no argument and pulls in the anchor, setting it in the bottom of the boat.

"Will you be leaving, then?" Celia asks as he dips the paddles back into the dark Sound. "Drive beneath the train trestle with one of three things?"

"What?" He pulls on the oars, and the boat glides into a swath of moonlight. "What are you talking about?"

"You aren't familiar with the local folklore? Lauren told me it last year after I'd gotten involved with someone here."

"Really, now … Let's hear it."

"She said that *everyone* who arrives at Stony Point

eventually leaves, driving beneath the stone railroad trestle with one of three things. A ring, a baby, or a broken heart."

"Huh." Shane glances toward the beach, then back to Celia. "Shit, that already happened, last time I was here. Years ago."

"So what was it?" Celia shifts on the bench, straightening her silver dress as she does. "What did you take with you beneath the trestle back then?"

"Left with a broken heart." He lifts the oars for a moment when they *drip, drip* into the sea. "The ring never got returned."

"Oh. Well, one out of three isn't so bad. I broke a record last year. You're looking at the first person in Stony Point history to go three for three."

Shane pulls on the oars and tips his head, watching her from beneath the brim of that cap of his. "A ring?"

Celia raises the sea-glass engagement ring from a chain around her neck.

Seeming to want a better look, Shane tips up his cap and leans forward to see the ring. Then? Then he lets out a low whistle. "And a ... baby?" he asks, picking up the oars again and paddling the boat closer to the channel into the marina. "The little one I met when I checked in at the inn? You were holding her?"

"Aria. My sweet Aria."

"So a ring. A baby ... *and* a broken heart?"

Celia only nods.

"Your husband broke your heart?" Shane asks. "What happened? Because I saw his picture in the old Foley's back room. When I had coffee earlier with Elsa."

"He wasn't my husband, but we came close." Celia lifts her necklace chain again. "This was my engagement ring."

"I don't get it."

"He was a sweet man, with heart issues of his own. He didn't survive his valve-replacement surgery." She gives a sad smile. "His name was Sal."

"Wait. Elsa's son?"

"That's right. Salvatore DeLuca. We were supposed to be married after his surgery. He gave me my sea-glass engagement ring right before he went in the hospital."

"So your baby? She's …"

"Yes," Celia whispers. "Aria is Sal's daughter. But Sal and I? We never made it to the altar."

Shane steers the wooden rowboat down the narrow channel and beneath a small bridge into the marina. "I am so sorry, Celia." He shakes his head and exhales a long breath. And still, nothing else as he pulls back on the oars. Until finally, "Now that? That's a damn shame."

"Aren't a lot of our stories here a damn shame?"

When Jason did it, when he held the cabin door open and told Kyle to *Do it*. To *Get the hell out and keep on walking*, he never expected what happened next.

Never expected Kyle to stare him down, then look away and blink back some tears of rage, or shame—hard to tell which. But Kyle clasped his hands behind his neck, took a long breath and ... apologized.

"It's been that kind of a day," he'd said, "when I don't even know what I'm saying anymore. Feel like I've been through the wringer. Which is why I'm at this little shanty. To *think*, before I mess up even more. To look at life from my cabin in the woods. You know, like—"

"Thoreau," Jason quietly finished. "Mitch mentioned that."

So after a groom-best-man-truce, they end up in the cabin's backyard. To think *and* talk. Quickly, though, to not keep Lauren waiting. But long enough to calm Kyle down before she shows up at his cabin door.

A few large tree stumps circle the firepit behind Chickadee Shanty. Jason sits on one of those stumps now as a small fire burns in the pit. Kyle doesn't sit, though. He's standing at the fire, watching the flames burn.

"And I was really trying to do that here. *Think*. Okay, Barlow? Because, yeah, Mitch told me to go to the cabin and just think. Like Thoreau did."

"That's it? Just think?" Jason asks, then takes a drag of a cigarette Kyle gave him.

"You got it. Damn, it's about as literary as I'll ever get. I sat in this quiet cabin, far, far away from the scene of the mess. And yeah, I was thinking. Until you arrived. At least, I was *trying* to think."

"What do you mean?"

"Well I didn't really think about Lauren, or about my marriage." Kyle sits on a tree stump, rests his elbows on his knees and gazes at the fire. "Just thought about Shane."

"No shit." Jason flicks the ash of his cigarette. "Like what?"

"Well, about one time in particular. Remember the night? About twenty years ago now? We went out in your little Whaler. You, Neil, me and Shane."

"Yeah. Your brother had gotten in trouble with some petty theft and was doing … community service, was it?"

"Yup. Shane was seventeen and still a minor. Caught a break and was issued community service, working with a mentor. On a lobster boat. That's when he fell in love with lobstering. Got his hands on one of those old wooden traps and taught us how to do it that night, too. We filled a bait bag, attached a buoy, dropped the trap in." Kyle stands again, walking near the flames. Behind him, lamplight spills from the windows of his little cabin, and shadows of tall trees surround it.

"I remember," Jason says, sitting back on his tree stump. "We went out past the rocks on the point. Threw that trap overboard and came back for it the next day."

Kyle lights a cigarette and exhales a stream of smoke. "Shit, my brother was doing community service and *still* breaking the law. Lobstering without a license."

"Hell, we were just kids. And pulled in a few bad boys in that lobster trap of his, too."

"Cooked them up the next night, all that fresh lobster. It was sweet." Kyle quiets then. The fire crackles, and a chorus of crickets chirps in the woods around them.

Jason shifts on his makeshift seat, lulled by that warm fire now.

"Those were good times, man," Kyle finally says. "Just,

I don't know. Easy." He paces around the firepit, and the flames cast his face in flickering shadows. "That's all I came up with, *ruminating* out here," he says, air-quoting the word. He takes a drag of his cigarette. "Thinking in the woods is so overrated. Thoreau could have it."

"It's not overrated. You had a nice memory. You and your kid brother were close once." Jason stands and flicks his half-smoked cigarette into the flames. "You saying you want to get back to that? Reconnect with him?"

"What?"

"Sounds like you're having second thoughts," Jason persists. "Like maybe you want to hash it out with him." He looks over at Kyle.

"Don't know."

"Yeah, tough call. Not sure you two are ready to gather 'round the campfire."

Kyle crouches in front of the firepit, his hands on his knees, his cigarette hanging from his fingers. "Ah, hell."

"What now?"

"I hate you, Jason Barlow," he says, taking another long drag of his smoke.

"Hate me?"

"Yeah. I hate you because you're always goddamn right." Kyle tosses his cigarette into the flames, too, then watches the sparks rise above the fire. "You say just the right shit to get me to change my stupid mind." He stands and drags a hand back through his recently cut hair, all nicely trimmed for his vow renewal. "Because you know something?"

"What's that?"

"I *have* been thinking about Shane lately. Even *before* all this mess today. So I don't know. Have him in my life again, like you're saying? Maybe? But then I get all pissed off about that stunt he pulled on me, and hell, it still stings. So … probably not. You know, fixing shit with him."

"Hey, man. I've always said that where Shane goes, so goes trouble. But look, you don't have to make any more decisions tonight, bro."

"One more, Barlow. I've got to try with Lauren and me. To get back to where we were. So get out of here, would you?" Kyle turns and heads to the cabin, about to open the screened back door. "Get out of here and send my wife in." Before stepping inside, he turns again. "And don't worry, I won't effin' blow it."

Jason motions for Kyle to wait up, then walks over to shake his hand.

But Kyle, well, Kyle pulls him into a hug.

So Jason slaps his big back before heading out around the little cabin to the dark parking lot. As he walks, he hears the cabin's screen door slam shut; smells the scent of pines rising tall in the woods; turns the corner and sees moonlight shining on the tiny lake where wild grasses whisper in the night.

fifteen

1:00 a.m. – Sunday

TWIGS AND LEAVES SNAP BENEATH their feet. The path to the cabin winds beside the dark woods, the tall trees blocking much of the moonlight. Slivers of it shine through the branches, the moonbeams shifting as the leaves rustle in a soft breeze. Pressed tight into the darkness is Chickadee Shanty, discernible in the night only by the golden lamplight in its paned windows. It's late now, and the crickets' song has quieted; the katydids' creaking call, slowed.

"I'll leave you here," Jason says when the porch stairs are within sight. He gives Lauren a hug, holding her close. "It's going to be okay, Lauren."

"Thanks, Jason," she whispers. "I hope so."

When he squeezes her hand and nods toward the cabin door, Lauren turns. She pauses and touches her fallen hair, then picks up her overnight bags and the small cooler.

From the shadows, Jason watches her go. Her sweatshirt hangs loose; her posture's tired; her hair still hangs on to that fallen chignon. But she presses forward, and when Jason sees the cabin door open, he turns back to his SUV. Kyle and Lauren are together. They'll work it out, come what may.

The *only* thing Jason wants to do then is get home. The only person he wants to see is Maris.

Tonight, for the first time in a long time, he feels the distance. Feels the long distance from the sea, the distance from his marriage. Right now, too many miles stand between himself and both.

So once in his SUV, he quickly picks up the highway. His headlights illuminate the gray pavement before him. Yellow reflectors line the center barrier; a hulking tractor-trailer traveling the opposite side is outlined with small lights; a lone car merges from an on-ramp in front of him; road signs almost blur at seventy miles per hour. There is only the hum of his tires on the pavement as Jason books it home.

⁓

But rolling over miles of pavement is conducive to something else. In the quiet hum of those tires on the road, in the occasional headlights of passing vehicles, Jason's *mind* is free to travel, too.

And travel it does—mostly to one thought in particular. He never got to raise a crystal glass and give Kyle his best man speech today, one that was going to be off the cuff.

Off the cuff, but a speech that was going to mention the driftline—much the way Kyle's speech did at Jason's own wedding to Maris two summers ago. Because Kyle nailed it that night in *his* best man speech. Right there on the Stony Point boardwalk, his was the most moving speech Jason's ever heard. Talking about the driftline, Kyle powerfully summed up how they were *all* connected through life's ups and downs.

Then when they learned *this* summer that Neil even titled his novel DRIFTLINE, the book Jason's own beautiful wife has taken on to complete, the word and all its meaning took on new significance. Especially after a day like today. So tonight—as the miles tick past, as the roads speed by—Jason's searching for the truth in that one word, and remembering Kyle's take on it, too …

"Okay, so years ago I read something in a book on beach life," Kyle had started his best man speech then. *"And I thought it appropriate tonight because heck, we're all beach friends, right? And what I read about was the driftline. Also known as the high tide line. We've all walked along it, that seaweed lining the beach. It's called a driftline because of everything that drifts in with the tide. If you give a good look, it's not just seaweed. There's sun-bleached shells, stones, driftwood, sea glass … all tangled in like little treasures.*

"Everything's connected, in the driftline, all those bits from the sea. And it reminds me of us, on grand days like today, when we're together

like this—Jason, Maris, me, Lauren, Eva and Matt." Kyle stepped forward and glanced down the boardwalk at the guests sitting at the tables. "Vinny and Paige, Nick, friends and family. Well, I think there's another driftline going on here at Stony Point. One with people and places and memories ... and I guess a little bit of heart twisted and tangled in, too, connecting us all.

"Even those who are gone are a part of this exclusive driftline." Kyle cleared his throat, then dropped his head for a long second before continuing. "I know full well that I'm standing in for someone tonight. Someone always a part of our own driftline. Someone we'd all give anything to have back." He turned to face Jason. "Your brother. Neil. I'm honored to stand in for him, but here's the thing. He's here, Jason. In that salty breeze coming off the water, in the sea fog in the shadows there." He nodded toward the end of the beach edged by the forest and rocky outcropping.

"But there's more, in our Stony Point driftline," Kyle began again. "Instead of seashells and stones and driftwood, we've got tears and laughter. And card games and stolen boats and Frisbee on the beach and good times at Foley's and swim races to the raft, and, and wisdom—God, do we have wisdom—connecting us all together."

―

Connecting us all together, Jason thinks now while driving. Snatches of Kyle's words return to him, words especially important today. Words that Jason remembers listening to while in his black tux and sitting on the boardwalk, Maris at his side. Words that deeply moved him that night. *Even those who are gone are a part of this exclusive driftline*, Kyle had said at Jason's wedding reception.

Which means that Shane Bradford is a part of that driftline, too. Like it or not. They'd denied that truth long enough, until they no longer could. Until today.

No, you don't always get to choose who or what washes up in life's driftline.

Driving the winding Connecticut roads, suddenly it happens again. The country landscapes and rural homes turn coastal. The shadowy night view becomes edged with winding saltwater marshes. Old shingled bungalows and swaying beach grasses beckon on cottage-lined streets.

Jason is on his way home.

Cliff couldn't be more relieved to sees lights on at the inn. From half a block away, lamplight shines in a few downstairs windows. So Elsa must be up. More importantly, the upstairs windows, where Shane's room would be, are dark.

Hurrying across the inn's parking lot, when Cliff sees that the kitchen light is also on, he heads to the side door. Wasting no time, he turns the knob and swings it open, nearly stumbling as he sweeps into the room. It takes a moment to catch his shaky breath, a moment for his eyes to acclimate after coming inside from the dark night.

But acclimate they do, to see Elsa wearing her turquoise caftan and sitting at her kitchen island. Pendant lights shine on many lace-wrapped Mason jars filled with sand and tea-light candles there. The decorated jars were meant to hang on the aisle chairs for the vow renewal—until Shane's arrival changed everything.

"You got him out of here?" Cliff asks, then pulls off his COMMISSIONER cap and drags his hand through his disheveled hair.

Elsa looks over at Cliff as she sorts the Mason jars. "Who? Kyle?"

"No, dagnabbit!" Cliff steps closer, worried now. "Shane."

"Yes. Yes, Cliff."

"Oh, thank God," Cliff manages as he sinks onto a stool at the marble-top island.

"He's taking a walk on the beach," Elsa continues as she aligns another Mason jar.

"*What?*" Cliff rushes to the window as if he could see even a scrap of the beach from here, especially at night. "No!" he insists, turning back and pointing vaguely to the parking lot. "He has to leave ... Jason was so mad ... That coffee has to get down the drain."

"Clifton?" In her sweeping caftan, Elsa walks to the sink and soaks a cloth with cool water. "Sit down. What's the matter with you, anyway?"

"Heck, I was supposed to do Jason a favor. But I've been waylaid all night! Someone took down half the speed barriers. Then there was a raccoon emergency, and a beached sailboat." Cliff drops onto a stool at the island again. "All that before my battery died."

"You're not making sense," Elsa tells him as she presses the folded cloth to his forehead. "I think you have a touch of heatstroke. Hold this."

Cliff does, holding the cool cloth to his face as Elsa pours a glass of cold orange juice. "Jason's going to wring my neck," he says, patting the cool cloth there, too.

"Are you seeing clearly? Drink this, it'll help."

Cliff takes the glass and gulps down the juice. "Be still my heart," he whispers as he sets aside the glass. "My old bones were not meant to jog."

"Jog?" Now Elsa sits beside him and touches his forehead. "You've been jogging? At *this* hour?"

"Yes! I had to get here in a hurry after my car battery died. All the way from—"

"Why didn't you call me?" Elsa touches her fingers through his mussed hair. "I'd have brought you that handy-dandy battery jumper I bought from one of those home shopping shows."

"Why didn't I call you? Because all I heard in my head was Jason's voice. *Get to Elsa's and pour that coffee down the fucking drain.*"

"Cliff! Your language!" Elsa says, getting up this time to heat a hunk of leftover vow-renewal lasagna in the microwave.

"Those are Jason's words, Elsa. Not mine. And that's not all," he adds as the microwave hums. "He said for me to throw my weight around and get Shane out of here."

"You know something?" From where she stands at the microwave, Elsa looks back at Cliff. "I had a couple cups of coffee with Shane. We had a real heart-to-heart tonight." Opening the microwave and pulling out the warm lasagna, she says, "And I think the kids are all wrong about him."

"Are you *kidding* me?" Cliff watches her while still catching his breath from his winded jog here—trying to beat the clock, beat Elsa's coffee chat with Shane, *and* come through for Jason.

"No. I'm serious."

"Oh, that Shane must've played you for a fool, my dear."

"No!" Elsa says as she sets the steaming lasagna in front of him, then gets a napkin and fork. "I can *read* people, Cliff."

"Read people?"

"Yes. By their mannerisms," she explains, sitting beside him again. "By their expressions, their body language. By their ... *way*. And I spent a lot of time talking to Shane tonight. About his life on the lobster boats, and about Stony Point, the inn. So I got my own vibes about him, instead of listening to everyone else. I could *read* him for myself." Elsa clasps Cliff's arm and gives a little shake. "Shane's *not* a bad person, I'm telling you."

"And you can tell Jason Barlow that, too." Cliff slices his fork through the cheesy lasagna. "Then you can *read* his reaction."

sixteen

1:10 a.m. – Sunday

WHEN KYLE OPENS THE CABIN door, the lamplight from inside spills out onto the porch.

Onto Lauren.

He sees nothing else. Not the moonlit lake beyond. Not the slatted rockers on the porch. Not the tall pines, whose heavy scent fills the night. Not shadows, not stars in the sky, not the stone bench set lakeside.

Just Lauren.

Just the worried shadows beneath her eyes. And the unzipped sweatshirt thrown on over her frayed denim shorts and black lace-up blouse. And the strands of blonde hair fallen from her pretty chignon.

What surprises him is how he has to briefly turn away with closed eyes—closed to press back sudden tears. Hot, stinging tears carrying every bit of the feelings of the day. Because every emotion squeezed from the past several hours has landed right here, right on the doorstep of Chickadee Shanty. Anger. Betrayal. Heartache. Regret. Love. Love's there, too. He presses a finger to his eye before looking at her again.

"Kyle, it's okay," Lauren says, taking a step closer. "Can we talk, please? I can explain."

"Don't." Kyle reaches out and gently presses his fingers over her lips. "Don't. Don't talk."

He takes Lauren's hand and instead leads her to the plaid sofa inside. The whole time—closing the door behind them, stopping to hang her sweatshirt on the antler coatrack, walking past the end tables covered with carved wooden chickadees—he doesn't let go of her hand. Even sitting on the sofa, he turns her hand in his, and with his other hand, drags a finger across her open palm. But he doesn't speak at first, because of the lump in his throat. If he tries to talk, oh that damn lump will twist up his words in some pathetic sob. Grief ... is what it feels like. Grief at his decision to cancel the vow renewal earlier. Grief at the thought of nearly losing this beautiful woman. Of hurting her. One choke-worthy lump holds it all.

So sitting in their cabin in the woods, instead of talking, Kyle silently traces her life line, her heart line, her fate line. Now there's something he's always believed in. Fate. He finds deep meaning in questions about what's destiny, what isn't. And Kyle's always believed they were destined to be together.

"I love you, Ell," he whispers hoarsely while drawing his finger across Lauren's fate line. "All I want is to stay with you." Still touching her hand, circling his finger on her palm, he looks at her. That's when his hand moves, when he lifts his finger to her chin and tips her face to his. "You and the kids are all I want. You're my world. Nothing will change that."

"I know that, Kyle." Lauren smiles briefly. "But you have to know why I—"

"No. You don't owe me another explanation. I heard everything you said today at home. The way I reacted, the way I went ballistic, I owe *you* the explanation. And an apology. Because I get it. I *get* it—what you did. I'm just sorry it took me this long to get it and that I couldn't see clearly before. Couldn't see *why* you invited my brother."

"Kyle, if I'd known Shane—"

He shakes his head, and she quiets, watching him.

They're too exhausted to find the words right now, so he has none. None that'll make a difference. None that'll take back his earlier anger, take back his decision to can their vow renewal today. None of his lame words would be good enough for his well-meaning wife, who invited Shane only out of the generosity of her heart.

All he has is himself.

Kyle raises his two hands to her face, leans close and gives Lauren the only thing he has left at the end of this eternal day. He scarcely, just barely, touches his lips to hers in the softest, most important kiss he's ever given. When he pulls back, he watches her weary eyes, and his thumb gently wipes a tear from her cheek.

seventeen

1:30 a.m. – Sunday

CELIA STOPS THE GOLF CART in front of the inn. "Thanks for helping with the flowers," she tells Shane as he gets out of the passenger seat.

"No problem, Celia. And thanks for that rowboat ride."

"Well, as assistant innkeeper, I at least hope you're enjoying your stay—brief as it is—at the Ocean Star Inn."

"More than you'd think. You and Elsa have been nothing but gracious." He tips his cap to her and gives a wave. "So take care now, and enjoy these summer days with your daughter," he quietly calls back as he walks to the inn's main door.

Celia watches him go, then steers the golf cart around back to the inn's gravel parking lot. She'll return the golf cart to Lauren tomorrow. But right now, Celia wants nothing more than to get out of her silver maid-of-honor dress and into comfy pajamas. Something soft, and loose, and cool. Maybe she'll have a cup of tea, too, after checking on Aria.

Walking across the inn's backyard to her little cedar-shingled gingerbread cottage, already she feels herself relax. The bungalow sits on a stone foundation, and from here, the diamond-shaped stained glass window glows from a light her father left on. She slows her step, though, and stops when she hears a peculiar sound. It has her look over toward where she dropped off Shane, this low, bluesy sound. But it's so faint, she has to be very still to really hear it.

After giving one last longing glance at her cottage, she turns and walks back through the yard. The dewy grass gets her sandals wet as she crosses the lawn, then moves along the side of the inn. Finally, in the dark, she looks around the corner and sees Shane on the front porch. She quickly steps back, out of sight, and presses her body flat against the shingled inn.

And okay, she listens to the quiet riff rising in the misty night. It's a sad enough sound to get her to peek around the corner again. In the shadows, Shane's sitting on the porch's top step. He's turned sideways, a knee drawn up as he leans against the railing post. But it's his hands that she notices now, they way they're cupped around a harmonica. The tune he plays is slow, and breathy, and what she hears is evidence of how the day feels. For her, anyway. Probably for everyone else, too—Shane included. In the harmonica's soft, slow vibrato, there comes an emotion that practically breaks her heart with the way it floats on the August night air. He plays the song so that it's barely audible, and the chilling effect is this: If anyone were to walk the sandy road past the inn at this late hour, they might think the night itself is weeping.

Celia listens a moment longer before walking back across the lawn to her cottage. She climbs the steps to her own porch, puts the key in the front door and does it. Yes, she looks back once more before turning the key and going inside.

From Eva's deck, the marsh seems different late at night. Quieter. More serious. Beneath the dampness rising off the sea, the salt air is more pungent. If it's true, if salt air really cures what ails you, Maris thinks each and every one of them needs a deep breath of it tonight.

The moon shines from high in the sky now, casting the marsh in pale light. Pale shadows, too. Shadows where Maris hears the tall grasses whispering, but can't really see them. It's how the day feels. Secretive. Mysterious. Everyone murmuring something behind a cupped hand, leaning close to someone else, whispering hushed words. Sitting out here beneath white lights glimmering at the patio table, and listening to the water splash against Eva's old wooden dock, the marsh grasses sighing, it's what Maris and Eva have been doing all evening. Sharing sister secrets.

Eva holds up the wine bottle and tips it to the side with a little shake. "Might as well kill the bottle," she says, then pours the last few drops into both their glasses.

"I'm so beat." Maris holds out her glass for Eva. "I'll finish this then get going. Hopefully it'll help me fall right asleep."

"It's late. Matt will drive you home, okay?"

Maris nods, then raises her wineglass. "Our last toast. To that blast from our past today," she says as Eva leans over and clinks glasses.

"More like a detonation from our past," Eva admits before taking a long sip of the wine. "The whole day blew up. I still can't believe Shane's even here. And that Lauren wants *you* to talk to him now."

"I know."

"Will you? Talk to Shane?"

"I don't know if that's a good idea." Maris tries taking a breath of that pungent salt air, but it doesn't seem to help much. "What would I even say?"

"You'd think of something, no? You always had a way with him," Eva reasons. "And maybe you *could* get him moving along. Because like Lauren said, he always listened to you."

Maris looks across the table at Eva. Her hair, which they'd curled earlier special for the vow renewal ceremony, hangs limp. Maris is sure hers does, too, as she tucks a strand behind her ear. "Imagine how Shane feels tonight. I mean, he was actually invited here, then the whole day imploded. We all must look so pathetic."

"Pathetic? Why?"

"Because none of us even reached out to him today."

Maris shifts in her seat, then draws a finger across the shoulder of the denim jacket she wears. Across the embroidered stars there. "None of us could bridge that horrible gap, even after all this time."

Eva leans across the table and whispers. "But Lauren really wants *you* to."

"Eva." Maris tips up her glass and finishes the remaining drops of wine. "The last time I talked to Shane Bradford, I was sobbing on that old payphone near the creek."

"That was a long time ago," Eva says. Her voice is as soft as the whispering marsh grasses. "And no one would hold it against you, Maris, if you saw him tonight. Since you're only helping Lauren."

Maris looks her sister straight on. "Jason might."

"Jason? But surely he understands that what happened between you and Shane back then has nothing to do—"

Maris is shaking her head, enough to stop Eva mid-sentence.

"Oh, no." Eva leans back and squints at her. "Please don't tell me …"

"That Jason has no idea Shane and I were once engaged to be married?" Maris gives a regretful smile. "That I sometimes think about Shane, and wonder what *ever* happened to him?"

"Maris!" Eva, yes, she does it. She gets up and hurries around the table to sit right beside her. "You *never* told Jason that you were engaged to Shane?"

"No. I never told anyone but you." Maris gets up and walks to the deck railing. Clusters of old painted lobster buoys, ironically, hang from the deck posts. She turns toward Eva still at the table. "Because remember that old pact we all made at Little Beach, around the bonfire one night?"

"Do I ever. Really, Maris. How full of ourselves were we, vowing to never utter Shane's name?"

"Regardless. That's what I did. Honored that bonfire vow and told no one Shane and I had been briefly engaged. Jason included," Maris tries to explain. "I didn't think it mattered anymore—mine and Shane's engagement. It was old history. Water under the bridge and we'd both moved on."

"Except now he's back."

"And after this really emotional day, I definitely don't need that little engagement secret to come out. *Especially* not tonight, on top of everything else." Maris looks out at the marsh, then sits beneath the deck umbrella strung with twinkly lights.

"But Lauren asked you to talk to him. Shane might listen to you," Eva persists.

"Maybe. Problem is, I really *don't* need Jason finding me talking to Shane, and then Shane saying something about our past."

"So what are you going to do?"

Pulling the cropped denim jacket tight around her shoulders, Maris leans back in her chair. She throws a glance up at the stars spattered across the sky over the distant beach. "What am I going to do?" Maris repeats. "I'm going to pray to *God* that by morning? Shane Bradford's long gone."

eighteen

1:40 a.m. – Sunday

CLIFF LOOKS OVER AT ELSA'S countertop. At her highfalutin fancy coffeepot, actually.

The one he was supposed to empty down the drain hours ago.

Before Elsa had any chance to chat with Shane Bradford.

The coffeepot sits there, shining pretty, all cleaned up now after Elsa put it to good use tonight, doing just that. Chatting while serving multiple cups of coffee to her guest. Cliff drags a piece of bread through the tomato sauce on his plate and simply groans.

"What's the matter?" Elsa asks.

"Answer me one thing. Just how long did you and Shane talk?"

"Like I said, for a few cups of coffee. A little more than an hour, at the very least."

Cliff can just imagine that talk. Oh, Elsa has that easy-breezy way about her. She could get a rock to talk, for crying out loud, the way she fusses and looks directly at your eyes when she's listening. The way she serves a delicious snack with the coffee. Maybe touches your arm after setting down the plate. The way she makes you feel that your words are the most fascinating she's ever heard.

But Cliff's no fool. What *really* draws people to her is that she means it. There's no phony act, no angle. Elsa's honest. She *is* fascinated by the stories people have. He's always loved that about her.

"Don't you think it odd, Cliff," she asks while taking his dish to the sink, "that none of the kids will even say what happened between Shane and Kyle?"

"Maybe. But maybe they have their reasons, too. And their hands are tied tonight, so they had no time for explaining."

"I suppose."

"All I know is that Jason made me swear to get Shane out of here. And I'm plenty sure Jason's got *his* reasons. Of which I'll never hear the end of now."

"Oh, *basta*! Enough, Cliff. We're all adults and all entitled to our own opinions of people." Elsa closes the dishwasher, dims the recessed lights and brings over a damp cloth.

"I'm just saying …" Cliff continues as Elsa sweeps that cloth across the marble island in front of him. "Shane must've done *something* to get everybody riled up. And we have to decide where our loyalties lie."

"Still. Since I don't *know* what happened between him

and his brother, I can't base my loyalty on it. Agreed?" Elsa asks when she sits beside him and picks up a biscotti from the glass dome on the island.

"But you don't really know *Shane*, either."

"I know enough." She nibbles at the pastry.

"And I know enough of what Jason asked me to do."

As he says it, Cliff swears he hears the inn's front door open. What he sees next confirms it. Shane Bradford, newsboy cap and all, waves to them as he walks past the kitchen doorway, apparently headed upstairs to his room.

"Hold on just a minute, Mr. Bradford," Cliff calls out as he gets off his stool and wipes his mouth with a napkin.

Shane backs up a few steps, stops in the doorway and looks at Cliff. "What can I do for you …" He pauses while eyeing the COMMISSIONER patch on Cliff's official Stony Point windbreaker. "*Commissioner*," he says while extending his hand for a shake.

"Cliff. The name's Cliff Raines," Cliff tells him. He extends his hand, pulls it back, then raises it again. "And I'll shake your hand, to seal an agreement."

Immediately Shane pulls his hand away. "Excuse me?"

"An agreement," Cliff explains, stepping closer with his hand still extended. "Right now. I'll shake if you agree to get out of here. Pack your bags and take off."

"Clifton!" Elsa says, rushing over from the marble-top island. "That's absurd!"

"No, it's not, Mrs. DeLuca." Cliff drops his hand and turns to her. "The rules are the rules, after all. And this inn is not open for business. Which means you're in violation of Ordinance B1. Conducting business in an unapproved location."

"My inn most certainly *is* approved," she insists while jabbing his official-jacket-clad shoulder.

"Not until Labor Day weekend." With his back to Shane, Cliff tries to give her an expression to just go with him, slightly tossing his head toward Shane behind him at the same time.

"Is something wrong with your eyes again?" Elsa asks.

Cliff just blows out a breath and turns to Shane, who is leaning in the doorway. Just like his brother, Kyle, it must be six feet of Shane standing there, filling the space. He nudges up his newsboy cap and watches Cliff and Elsa with some obvious amusement.

"Well." Cliff turns up his hands. "I must insist you leave, Mr. Bradford. Regardless of Mrs. DeLuca's argument, your staying is in violation of Stony Point ordinances. And as commissioner, it's my responsibility to enforce them, *or* issue fines."

"But Cliff. It's so late," Elsa declares while pointing to a round wall clock trimmed in old fisherman's rope. "It's one forty-five in the morning!"

"And it's *time* I showed Shane the door," Cliff persists.

Because Cliff knows. It's now or never. If the decision swings to *never*, Jason Barlow will *never* let him forget it. And then some. So Cliff hitches his head toward the inn's main door.

"I had no way of knowing about your ordinance, Commissioner Raines." Shane, not moving from his doorway post, crosses his tattooed arms in front of him. "My vow renewal invitation stated that guests would be accommodated at the Ocean Star Inn. So you need to redirect your warning and fines to Mrs. DeLuca? Or maybe to Lauren?"

"Boys, boys." Elsa motions them into the room, over to the kitchen island sparkling beneath those recessed lights. The low lighting in the room is inviting, and comforting, this late at night. "Sit down and we'll talk about this. I have some Italian cookies, and I'll ... I'll make a pot of decaf." With her caftan sweeping behind her, she rushes to the counter.

"Elsa," Cliff says, not fooled by the evocative lighting's ambiance, and the aroma of fresh-ground coffee beans. His voice drops in all seriousness. "Do you remember what I said about *coffee* earlier?"

"Clifton!" She turns on the kitchen faucet while saying over her shoulder, "Don't you dare repeat that in front of our guest."

"And ... And there will be no cookie swindling, either," Cliff informs her. "Now go get your battery charger, woman!"

"*Woman?*" Shane asks from his doorway post.

Elsa shuts off the tap and walks out of the room. "It's in my utility closet," she says as Shane moves aside to let her by.

"Elsa," Shane says, gently taking her arm. "You don't have to answer to this man."

"He's just full of hot air. It's okay." Elsa pats Shane's

hand so that he relinquishes his hold. "And his car needs a jump-start," she explains while opening the nearby closet door.

With Elsa busy banging around in that closet now, Cliff zips his windbreaker and puts on his official gold-stitched, black COMMISSIONER cap. Maybe it'll help throw his authority around.

"By the way, Cliff," Elsa's muffled voice carries to the kitchen. "I *am* in my pajamas." Another thudding bang, then her voice getting clear as she closes the closet door. "And you know how I feel about women going outside in their pajamas."

"I'll go with him, Elsa," Shane says, taking the battery and cable from her. "It's very late. You should stay in now."

Okay, so Elsa won't let this gentlemanly gesture pass without notice. When she looks at Cliff with a raised eyebrow, he reads it, that eyebrow. He sees her direct gaze, too, insisting Shane is a *good* person. Someone who cares about what's going on all around him.

Cliff turns up his hands. "Fine. Let's go then, Mr. Bradford."

"Why don't you take my car and drive there?" Elsa asks. "Shane can drive it back once you get your car started."

"No need, Elsa. I'll drive us over in my truck," Shane tells her.

But Cliff's already hurrying down the hallway to the front door, which he's opening as Shane offers to drive. Even that'll take too much time, getting settled in his vehicle. All that matters is that the sooner Shane follows him out of the inn, well, the sooner Cliff will succeed in accomplishing his mission for Jason.

"I'll walk," Cliff yells to them. "I need to cool off, anyway."

When he hurries down the porch stairs, he glances back to see Shane waving to Elsa.

Elsa, who is standing in the doorway while watching Cliff walk out into the night with Shane.

He should be in bed. In bed and sound asleep. All of them should be. Cliff walks the sandy beach road toward the street where his car is as dead as its battery. He hears footsteps gritty on the pavement behind him as Shane trots along to catch up.

"Did I miss something back there?" Shane asks, looking over his shoulder once he's beside Cliff.

"What do you mean?" Cliff keeps a steady gaze ahead.

"Seriously, Commissioner. Elsa mentioned being widowed. But you two are like an old married couple. Is Elsa *your* wife now?"

Cliff can't help it then, the way the question stops him in his tracks. Just for a second or two before he continues on his night walk. "No. But she's my lady, okay? I've been ... wooing her."

"Wooing?"

"Yes. Wooing." Cliff turns up his hands. "You know. Trying to win her over by making loving gestures."

"I'm not sure Elsa's feeling it." Shane looks back toward the inn again, shaking his head as he does.

What can Cliff say? Nothing. He doesn't owe Shane an explanation. But he damn well might owe Jason Barlow an explanation if Shane's still here at daybreak. As long as Cliff gets this scoundrel out of here by then, he figures Jason will be okay. He'll simmer down.

That sliver of hope lowers Cliff's blood pressure. So together, he and Shane quietly walk the cottage-lined roads. Many of the beach homes are dark now. At others, lanterns illuminate front doorways. Some folks linger over a card game, or with a late-night drink, on screened porches. Cliff hears ice clink in their glasses; hears voices talking and softly laughing. Beneath the misty moonlight, sweeping hedges of ornamental dune grasses become hulking shadows. Damp beach towels strung from a rope beneath a tall maple tree hang limp. An illuminated lighthouse statue stands in a flower garden.

"Where's your car, Commissioner?" Shane asks as they veer toward the parking lot behind the boat basin.

"Over on Sea View Road. We can cut through here to the footpath."

"You live on Sea View?"

"What? No." Cliff pictures the Stony Point Beach Association trailer that he secretly calls home. "No," he says, deflecting the question. "There's a sailboat beached on the rocky bluff on Sea View. The vessel will be lifted off by crane in the morning. But when I got the initial call, I parked my car there and left the headlights on to illuminate the danger area. You know," he says, looking over to Shane as they cross the empty parking lot, "so I could better assess the situation."

"Let me guess. And you killed your car battery at the same time."

"Bingo. By the time I got the area taped off, my headlights and battery were kaput."

"Yo, boss!" a familiar voice calls out. "Is that you, Commish?"

Cliff shields his eyes and looks toward the marina. A car is backed halfway down the boat ramp.

"I've been looking for you," the voice continues as a man comes around the vehicle. "Could really use a hand."

"Ah, criminy," Cliff quietly says as he veers toward the boat basin. "What's the problem, Nicholas?"

"Well, the first problem is that you won't bump me up on the waiting list for a vacant boat slip. Because I've been patrolling the coastline for Kyle, and without a slip of my own, now I have to tow my boat out of the water." Nick turns and motions to his waiting Whaler. "I tied it in a vacant slip temporarily, until I could back my trailer in. Come on, I could use some assistance. Another pair of hands to help get her out."

"Right now?" Cliff asks, walking closer.

"Sure. When I got the text that Jason found Kyle, I was out past the point. Took me this long to get back."

Cliff, upon mention of Jason and Kyle, looks at Shane behind him. Wearing his newsboy cap, he's standing in shadow. But he also lifts the battery and cables he's holding, seeming impatient to get moving.

Nick bends to the side to see past Cliff. "Oh. Kyle! Didn't notice you there."

"Not Kyle," Shane answers, walking closer.

"Whoa." Nick squints through the shadows. "Hell, you look just like him. Sorry about that. So, how you doing?" he asks, approaching and shaking Shane's hand. "You the new security guard?"

"No. I'm Kyle's brother."

"No shit. Shane?" Nick asks, looking over to Cliff, then back at Shane. "You're the dude? Hey, good to meet you."

Cliff clears his throat and checks his watch. This here is another instance of being waylaid, and if these instances keep piling up, Jason just won't believe him. Plus, Cliff will never get home to catch some much-needed sleep. "Nick," he says. "Shane and I are on our way to a ... *situation*. Can't you get someone else to help you? Vinny, maybe?"

"Commissioner." Shane hands Cliff Elsa's portable battery and jumper cables. "I'm on boats every day of my life."

"Seriously?" Nick asks.

"I've been told Shane's actually a lobsterman, Nicholas," Cliff says.

"Awesome. Where do you work? Around here?"

"No, Connecticut lobstering's really on the downswing. I live up north. Rockport, Maine. And Cliff?" Shane motions to Nick's Whaler docked in someone else's slip. "This here is nothing. I'll help Nick get his boat trailered in no time. It'll take ten minutes, tops."

Ten long minutes, when all Cliff wants to do is keep a promise to Jason Barlow. With an eye on both his watch *and* on the boat basin maneuverings, Cliff feels every one of those ten minutes tick past.

Ticking as Nick unhitches and backs his boat out of the slip.

Ticking more as Shane gets in Nick's car and backs the trailer deeper down the boat basin ramp.

Still ticking when Shane gets out of the car and motions Nick to *Steer left. A little right now.*

Tick-ticking as Nick positions his boat, aligns it and drives it up onto the waiting trailer.

"Easy does it," Shane tells him as the hull comes out of the water. Shane moves in front of the boat, hooks the winch on, ratchets it up and connects the bow safety chain. "You're good," he calls out, prompting Nick to shut off the boat's engine.

Cliff watches it all as a night mist settles over the moored boats in the marina. The mist looks like a thin fog, hovering over the water. Finally, once that little Whaler's engine is shut off, Nick hops off the boat and shakes Shane's hand again.

"Thanks, man. I got it from here."

"You sure?" Shane asks.

"Yep. You saved me a lot of aggravation doing that myself. I'll finish up now."

"Sweet little vessel you got yourself. Glad to help."

Doggone it, Shane was right. Took no more than ten minutes. As Shane turns to Cliff and says, "Let's go,

Commissioner," Cliff checks his watch to be sure. Squints closer at it, then looks over at Nick securing his boat on the trailer. Then looks at Shane.

"Ten minutes," Shane says as he heads toward the footpath. "Flat."

nineteen

2:20 a.m. – Sunday

THE DOG IS AS TROUBLED as everyone else today. Once Jason's home, she's at him, pestering him, following him. The German shepherd whines some, and leaves a sloppy lick on his hand when he's standing at the kitchen counter to plug his phone into its charger.

"Maddy!" Jason says, giving his wet hand a shake. "Settle down."

But he knows she won't; not until he does. So he ignores her as he unbuttons the top two buttons of his dress shirt and untucks it from the wrinkled best-man pants he still wears. A mug half filled with cold coffee sits beside the sink. Did that really happen today, his drinking coffee and waiting for Kyle to arrive to put on his groom threads? His looking out the window for Kyle's beat-up pickup?

Harder to believe, just three days ago, Maris had turned on their jukebox and they danced outside on the deck, beneath the stars. *We never stop loving someone, even after they're gone,* she'd said when she saw how bothered Jason was by a celebration, *any* celebration, happening this year. Happening ten years after the horrific motorcycle accident that changed everything. *So ... let this be the summer of love, Jason,* she'd whispered while they slow-danced in the shadows. *For Neil, for Kyle and Lauren. For yourself.*

Tiki torches flickered around them that warm evening. A warm evening that ended in their bedroom, where Maris put an end to Jason's self-pity. Where she knelt down and gently removed his prosthetic leg. Where he apologized for being a self-centered ass. Where she forgave him with her touch. Where he traced a finger along her jaw and wondered what he ever did to deserve her. Where they made love, and she convinced him to live his life *today*—not in the past.

During that night, a night as dark as this one, Maris gave him his sweet summer back.

Which is why Jason bought overloaded ham and salami grinders earlier today. And set them out with a couple of cold beers while waiting for Kyle to arrive. The groom and best man were going to have lunch together and toast the vow renewal. All because Maris convinced Jason this could be a summer of love, not a summer of mourning.

So he felt ready to commemorate Kyle and Lauren's ten-year anniversary. Sipping a hot coffee at lunchtime, he checked his watch; he looked out the window for any sign of the happy groom.

It's the same coffee cup he set down beside the sink after getting Lauren's text. After reading her words saying,

Oh my God, Jason. Please come over. And that text message put a quick and decisive end to the celebratory day going anywhere near as planned.

Now, Jason tosses the coffee dregs down the drain and puts that cup in the dishwasher. After shutting off the kitchen light Maris left on for him, he opens the fridge. There's got to be something to eat, some leftover to heat in the microwave. Some midnight—he pauses with a glance at the wall clock—change that to some two-thirty-in-the-morning snack. Closing the refrigerator, he goes into the dining room and turns on the lantern-chandelier. Maybe some pastry is wrapped on the sideboard. Some plastic-wrap covered, day-old caramel-drizzled brownie.

But there's nothing. Nothing more than a bouquet of dried marsh grasses and cattails spilling from a ceramic pitcher. And two pillar candles set on silver pedestals. A few liquor bottles, too—wine and such.

Jason sits at the painted farm table and brushes through a few pieces of mail, then sets them aside with another glance at the server. Nope, no food there.

Glances up at the ceiling where Maris must be in bed and sound asleep by now. No wife to talk to, either.

He drags a knuckle along his scarred jawline. Nothing. No food, no talk.

But when he gets up, a bottle of Scotch on the sideboard catches his eye.

"That'll do," he says to himself. Then he half fills a heavy tumbler, shuts off the lantern-chandelier and goes into the living room, where Maris also left on a dim light. Of course, the dog is at his heels the entire time. But it's as if Maddy knows. As soon as she senses he's headed for the upholstered chair in the corner, she steps into her dog bed beside it. Twice she turns around, curls into the cushioned bed, then rests her muzzle on the edge of it, keeping an eye on him.

Before sitting, Jason walks to the mantel over the stone fireplace. He picks up the framed photograph from his wedding two summers ago. Wearing his black tux, he waltzes with Maris on the evening sand. The horizon is violet over the water; tiki torches and candles in Mason jars flicker on the sand around them.

Just like the night was supposed to be for Kyle and Lauren. There should've been sunset dances at the water's edge; champagne toasts beneath the stars; good food at the inn; friends and love filling the summer night.

Jason lights one of the hurricane lanterns on the mantel, then takes the whiskey glass to his chair and finally, finally sits. Before dropping his head back and closing his eyes for a long moment, he first shuts off the table lamp beside him and sits in relative darkness. With only the lantern flickering on the mantel, and with a soft glow coming from their jukebox in the alcove, the living room turns sepia. It's all shadows and shapes: the furniture, and lamps, and seaside paintings hung on faded walls needing a coat of paint. Everything is indistinguishable in the dim light.

What the hell was today all about? Sipping his Scotch,

Night Beach

Jason wonders how the day changed from one thing to another, completely—yet nobody saw it coming. They were all purely blind to it.

His hand tugs out the silver chain around his neck until he holds his father's Vietnam War dog tags. He feels the dings and scratches in them. Sitting in the dark, Jason drags those old dog tags along the chain, back and forth, all while remembering his father's low voice. While thinking of his serious tone when a memory from the jungles was being shared.

Because today? Everyone here at Stony Point was blind to something coming right at them. For the love of God, no one—not one of them—saw the day's turn rolling right at them. Didn't see a glimpse, a shadow, a hint. Nothing. Just like the night blindness his father used to talk about.

One story in particular he'd only tell his sons outside, when they'd sit together on the stone bench on the bluff on moonless nights. The sky had to be as black as the sea; so black, it was hard to see your hand in front of you. All your other senses kicked in, instead. You could feel the sea damp. Smell the salty breeze. Hear the waves break. But sight? This story was told when they had little.

"I'm not sure which was worse, boys," their father would begin. "Waking up and seeing only blackness, or the *panic* that followed. Because, shit, the darkness was *so* deep that you couldn't see past it and truly *believed* you were blind. That something had happened in the godforsaken jungle that stole all your sight."

"*Get up.*"

Jason's father always began the story with those two words. Then, after being quiet for a moment—like he must've been when it happened in 'Nam—he went on. *I didn't know who said it,* his father explained to them. *There was just a sudden voice, quiet and close to my ear. My eyes opened, but that's all that moved. The rest of my body was stone-still. We had stopped for the night in the side of an embankment. It was covered in vines and dirt, but we dug in and had some cover.*

"*Get up.*"

In my exhaustion, I'd fallen so deep asleep, I couldn't even be certain there was a voice at all. Did I really hear it? As I lay there, listening, all I heard were the God damn bugs. It was one solid screeching sound. And some animal call, too, in the mix. Hoyee. Hoyee. Every now and then. A jungle cat? Or some distressed pheasant? Maybe.

Or was it?

Because it could also be a VC mimicking one of the animals. The Viet Cong did that, tricking the enemy. Duping us. Lulling us into a false sense of security.

Still I didn't move. Only my eyes were open and seeing nothing. Nothing at all. Just blackness. The trees in the jungle blocked out any starlight, the moon. It's like there was no sky at all, and only the night pressing down on me.

Again, I heard the voice. "Get up, soldier." Except this time, the words came with a light shove to my back. "We're on the move."

So I had to instantly orient myself. I'd fallen asleep with my helmet on, pants tucked into my boots to keep the bugs out. The leeches, especially. My weapon was right there, too, practically beneath my arm. The only way I knew all this, though, was by touching my head. My legs. By groping around in the ditch we'd dug. And around me, a few other soldiers were shuffling too. I could hear their movement. Whispers.

Then, closer ... Hoyee. Hoyee.

And everyone stopped with that sound.

So that was the danger.

Serious enough that the same hand that shoved me now grabbed hold of my arm and yanked me up. "Let's go."

"Wait." Oh, my eyes. They were wide open. Open and blinking. Again, then again. But they wouldn't work. I tried to open them wider, but nothing. I squeezed them shut in a tight blink, over and over. All my damn eyes could see was black. Thick black. For all I knew, I'd walk straight into the VC camp. "I can't see, man. I can't see," I whispered as loud as I dared.

"Shit," the soldier who'd hit me said. "You'll be all right. You'll be all right."

I reached my arm wildly around, trying to touch some familiar landmark, some tree or thick vine or roots. "I'm not fucking kidding, man. I'm blind." When I said it, I panicked and stumbled, catching myself from falling by touching ground with my hand.

"Listen. It's just night blindness. It'll go away when your eyes adjust and your night vision kicks in." He took my hand and I felt him give a shake. "We can't stop, man. They're too close, the VC. Here, grab the back of my shirt. Don't let go, either. Just keep moving with me." No sooner did I desperately clutch a handful of his shirt fabric, than he said one more thing as he maneuvered the jungle brush—the twigs and leaves swiping my face, branchlets snapping back at me like a whip. "Just keep staying alive."

"And I did," his father told them out on the bluff. He'd motion to the dark sky over the sea, the two indistinguishable from each other. "I put one booted foot in front of the other in the muck, picked up my knees practically to my chin just to get through the tangled vines. Felt some monster spider cross my cheek one furry leg at a time. Trusted my comrade in front of me and didn't let go of his shirt. Not for one petrified second. Even after my eyes finally adjusted and things took vague shape in the night, I held on and groped my way through."

Jason runs a thumb over his father's metal dog tags.

Right now, in Jason's own world, everyone is panicked. Blindsided. Stumbling. Kyle and Lauren. Maris. Cliff and Elsa. Celia. All of them, himself included.

Groping their way through one black night, holding on to whoever's near them, to whatever they possibly can.

twenty

2:30 a.m. – Sunday

"YOU REALLY THINK THIS PORTABLE charger will juice your battery?" Shane asks when they approach Cliff's stranded security car.

"We're about to find out." Cliff circles the car, which is still parked at an angle halfway across the street. A nearby streetlight throws some illumination on the stalled vehicle. "Pop the hood," he tells Shane.

While he waits, Cliff plugs the jumper cables into the charger. Once the hood is open, he sets the charger beside the car battery and pulls folded instructions from his pocket.

"Attach red clamp to positive terminal," he whispers, glancing at the battery, "and black clamp—"

"I got it." Shane suddenly appears, leans over and takes hold of the jumper cables.

Dagnabbit, Cliff thinks while Shane attaches the clamps

to the dead battery's terminals. If Barlow ever saw this, saw Shane Bradford tinkering over his car engine, there'd be hell to pay. Funny though, how this Shane reminds Cliff of his son, Denny—who's always reaching into engines at the car shows they attend together. Spends half his time bent over beneath some GTO or Camaro hood, maybe straightening only to finish a hot dog, or to sip from a cold beer.

"Now what?" Shane asks while fussing with the clamps and throwing a glance at Cliff.

"Well, it says here …" Cliff pauses, moving the instructions further out and squinting. "Says to press the jump-start button on the charger."

Shane does just that, then turns and walks toward the driver's side. "Done," he says over his shoulder.

"Not yet!" Cliff calls as Shane gets in the car. "We're supposed to—" Before he can finish, Shane turns the key in the ignition, but … nothing.

"Doesn't work," Shane tells him as he leans out the driver's door.

"You didn't give me a chance to read the rest. Says here to *wait* for the blinking light to go *solid*."

"I'll try again."

"Hang on!" Cliff yells. "We've also got to wait between attempts. That flashing green light indicates the safety check is underway. Need the light to go solid, for the safety check to complete first." As he watches the pulsing light, Cliff reaches into his jacket pocket and pulls out his scuffed-up domino. He gives it a spinning toss, right then and there in the street, then snatches it midair.

"What's that?" Shane asks.

"This? Why, this here's my lucky domino." Cliff walks over to the open driver's door and tosses the domino to Shane. "Things always seem to go my way when it's nearby."

Shane turns the domino over in his hand. "Is that right? How so?"

"Long story ... Actually? End of story," Cliff tells him as he takes back his domino. "But watch this," he says, then rubs the domino between his hands before leaning into the car and carefully propping it on the dashboard—in plain sight for Shane to witness. "Good luck in-action is about to commence."

"You believe in that talisman shit?" Shane asks. Still sitting in the car, he picks up the domino and tries a toss himself.

"Give it a lucky flip—really get it spinning—then put it there. Right on the dash."

Shane nods and gets out of the car to give the domino a flipping spin high in the air beneath the streetlight. After catching it in one swoop, he gets back in the car and carefully stands Cliff's good-luck domino dead center on the top of the dashboard.

"Now see for yourself," Cliff calls out as he hurries back to the engine and battery charger and jumper cables beneath that propped-open car hood. "Okay, solid green light on the charger. Give it a go!" he yells. When the engine turns over and nicely rumbles, he gives Shane a thumbs-up. "Hot dog, it worked."

"You're all set, then." A few moments later, Shane walks over in the darkness and gently slams shut the hood before slapping the top of it. "I left the car running so you'll get home safely. Don't turn the engine off till then. Let that battery get juiced."

"Will do."

"Okay. So I'll be on my way now," Shane says with a tip of his newsboy cap as he turns away.

Nodding, Cliff walks around his nicely purring car—but hesitates. Because now he gets it, gets what Elsa said earlier. That Shane, well, he's been nothing but personable. Cliff has no reason to dislike him. He glances over at Shane walking alone toward the inn. He's got on a long-sleeved button-down over a tank, and that cap of his, too. But still, the night air's pretty damp now. And it's dark, which is when the critters—raccoons and skunks—prowl. What can it hurt to give the guy a ride? The only one who'd have a beef with it is Jason. And Jason—who must be sound asleep by now in his big old cottage on the bluff—will never know the difference.

"Ah, heck," Cliff says as he opens the driver's door. He puts the car in gear, pulls up beside Shane and lowers his window. "Just get in and I'll give you a lift. I'm headed that way anyway, bringing the charger back to Elsa."

"Much obliged, Commissioner," Shane tells him after circling the car and settling into the passenger seat.

At this late hour, the few lampposts still lit have a halo of misty air around them. The moon is hazy too, rising far over the sea. But the cottages are mostly dark now, shuttered for the night.

"That still the Barlow place?" Shane asks when they pass a gabled cottage further down on Sea View, near the bluff.

"It is." Cliff looks over. The cottage sits high on a stone ledge. He can clearly see it, as the house rises in silhouette against the moonlit night sky. Low limbs of a maple tree sweep along the side porch. A few paned windows are dimly lit. "Jason and Maris' place now. Jason's got his barn studio out back, and Maris works in her writing shack there, too."

As he tells Shane this, Cliff remembers Jason's one order from earlier this night: *Pour that coffee down the fucking drain and get Shane out of there.* So a new panic overtakes Cliff. Here he is, right outside the Barlow house, for God's sake. What's the matter with him? Is he *looking* for trouble? Because that's what he'll surely have, a heaping dose of it, should Jason *not* be asleep and instead drive up right about now. So Cliff guns it and takes the next sharp turn.

"Inn's thataway," Shane reminds him, pointing left.

"I know damn well where the inn is. We're taking a detour."

When Shane tosses up his hands, what Cliff doesn't say is that still—no matter what, no matter how helpful Shane has been—Cliff *has* to eventually report to Jason that Shane is gone. Coming that close to the Barlow residence was a cruel reminder. There's too much risk involved if he doesn't get Shane out of here; Cliff and Jason had a gentleman's agreement to do so, after all. If Cliff breaks the agreement, what it'll all boil down to is this: It'll put his secret identity as Sailor on the line.

An identity that only Jason is aware of.

An identity being kept confidential by *another* gentleman's agreement—that one made only yesterday afternoon in a rowboat. What Cliff thought would be a routine practice run of paddling from the boat basin to the vow-renewal site further down the beach turned into something else when Jason boarded the boat.

Turned into a tell-all, out in that rowboat. There, Cliff revealed to Jason the true story of that mysterious neighborhood boy named Sailor. Yes, Cliff admitted to Jason that *he* was in fact Sailor, the little boy Carol Fenwick's grandfather valiantly died for while searching for him in a hurricane. Afterward, with a simple handshake, he swore Jason to secrecy.

And Cliff's sure that *one* broken agreement will prompt another. Meaning that if he doesn't get Shane out of here tonight, his cover will be blown. Jason might be mad enough to break the *other* handshake agreement—resulting in Cliff's true identity as little lost Sailor being revealed to all.

Which would cause enough anguish for Cliff to leave Stony Point behind, for good.

"Listen, Shane," Cliff persists as he begins a meandering drive along the winding beach roads. He needs a few minutes to present his case. "You seem like a nice enough fellow—helping people out, having friendly talks. But you showed up here and folks all ran scared-like. The day fell apart." He glances over at Shane sitting silently beside him. "Just so you know," Cliff continues as he turns onto another narrow road and slowly maneuvers around the speed blocks, "everyone would have me believe you're bad news. But here's the thing. Prior to becoming commissioner of this beach community, I spent my career as a judge in family court for this fine state of Connecticut. And believe me, I've heard it all. Divorce, custody, abuse, juveniles involved in illegal behavior. So whatever happened between you and your brother, I've heard it. Problem is … no one here's talking. So tonight, I'm asking you. What happened with you and Kyle?" When he slows the car and glances over at Shane, Shane simply shakes his head. "You're not going to tell me either, are you?"

"No, sir. The person I'd *like* to talk to, though, is Lauren."

"Lauren?"

"That's right. Because Lauren reached out to me with an invitation, and it'd be a damn shame if I couldn't have a few words with her before I leave. Make sure all's okay. Like I've said, I'd never have just shown up here without her invite."

Cliff takes a left and cuts through to Hillcrest Road. The cottages on this street are pressed close together—painted bungalow to weathered colonial to Nantucket-style. "I don't even know where Lauren is right now," Cliff admits.

"That's fine. She's probably too shook up to even think straight, after losing her vow renewal day." Shane takes a long breath and draws his hand along his whiskered chin. "But … listen. If I leave you a letter, do you think you could get it to her? Not right away, but in a few days. You know, after the dust settles and she can read it with a clear head."

"Well, I suppose I could." Cliff looks over at Shane again before turning off Hillcrest, then driving up and down a few more cottage-lined roads. The cottages are nothing more than hulking shadows against the night sky now. Lights have been shut off; heads rest on pillows; dreams, sweet dreams ensue.

Oh, if only it were him, sound asleep on his futon in that metal trailer.

If only it were him slumbering, the troubles of the day at bay.

If only he weren't bargaining with one who some might call the devil.

With a sigh, Cliff agrees. "Yes, I could deliver a personal note for you. That seems reasonable enough. Do you have the letter at the inn?" Cliff asks.

"No. I was actually hoping to see Lauren earlier. Which never happened. Guess I *could* send an email, but that seems too impersonal. So I thought a letter would be good. I'll have to write something when we get back."

"Here's what I can do." The Ocean Star Inn is only a block away, so Cliff's running out of time. He has to make his case for Shane to actually leave here—once and for all—and leave fast. "Get that letter written, and bring it to the Stony Point Association office. You know where it is … in the trailer before the train trestle. Just leave your envelope in the mailbox outside. And I'll do that for you, Shane. I'll get your letter to Lauren sometime next week. But …" Cliff says when he finally, *finally* pulls the car into

Elsa's driveway at the inn. "I'm asking you a favor, too."

"Kind of figured that was coming."

Cliff parks, but leaves the engine running to keep the battery charged until he gets home. "I'm not kicking you out, like I tried before," he says while looking through the windshield toward the inn. The kitchen windows are illuminated, so Elsa must be waiting up for them. "No. This time, I'm *asking* you to leave here. And right away." He holds up his open hand to stop Shane from arguing. "Hear me out."

"Go ahead," Shane says between his teeth.

"My reason is that if you stay on at the inn, Elsa will take the full brunt of everybody's wrath." Now, *now* Cliff looks at Shane, directly. "They *won't* let up on her, either. Believe me. And Elsa doesn't deserve it. The past year has been harder on that poor woman than most people experience in a lifetime. Elsa's had complete and true heartache, losing her only son."

"Sal."

"That's right. So whatever's gone down between you and your brother, well," Cliff says with a nod toward the inn, "the fallout should *not* be put on her."

"I can understand that. Elsa's a sweet lady."

"And a very special person. So we have a deal? I'll deliver your letter to Lauren. But in exchange, I'm *asking* you to leave, right away. For Elsa's sake."

Shane does it then. He extends his hand, and in the dark car, they shake on it.

Elsa reads the text message she just received from Celia. *I'm home in the guest cottage, finally in my PJs and turning in.*

Okay, glad to know this. What a night, Elsa types back.

A sad one, Celia answers. *But all's good here, Aria sleeping soundly. Goodnight now. Stop by for coffee in morning with me and Dad before he heads back.*

While typing her reply, Elsa hears Cliff's car turn in. The tires crunch over her crushed-stone driveway before the car comes to a stop.

Then? No slam of a car door. Nothing. Which gets Elsa to send her text, set down her phone, press aside a curtain and look out the window. Cliff is still in his car, and though she can't see in the dark, she assumes Shane is with him.

Still, nothing. So they must be talking about something. While she waits, Elsa nudges straight a thin starfish propped in the window.

But the car doors remain closed. Seems that *everyone's* trying to get at the root of the Shane and Kyle conflict, even Cliff. Because what *else* could he be jabbering about at this ungodly hour? When the two men finally emerge from the car, she hurries to the inn's door and lets them inside.

"Everything work out with your battery, Cliff?"

"Yes, perfect. What would I do without you, Elsa?" He pulls her close and leaves a light kiss on her cheek. "Let me put this back in your utility closet," he says, holding up her portable charger and jumper cables.

"I made a fresh pot of tea, Shane," she says when Shane comes in and closes the door behind him. "I hope you'll take a cup upstairs to unwind."

Cliff's muffled voice rings out from the closet. "That's good. He can have it while he packs his bags."

"Cliff! It's three in the morning!" Elsa exclaims back at him. "If he leaves now, he'll fall asleep at the wheel."

"That's okay, Elsa." Shane takes her hand in his and clasps it with the other. "I'll pack tonight, grab some sleep and leave first thing, right with the sunrise. Be gone before you even get up."

"Are you *sure*?" Elsa tips her head, watching him. He looks tired, and a few hours' sleep might not be enough rest for the long drive back to Maine. "You *did* book a reservation for the entire weekend."

"I'm sure. And thank you for your hospitality during my stay. I won't forget it." With that, Shane tips his newsboy cap. "But I also don't want to cause you any more trouble with folks around here, so it's best that I take off."

"Well, come in the kitchen and get a cup of tea to bring upstairs. You too, Cliff."

"None for me," Cliff tells her as he closes up the utility closet. "I'm leaving now. Been a long night, and my engine's still running to keep the battery charged." He looks past her toward Shane. "Shane?" he asks, giving a salute. "Thanks for your help tonight. You take care of yourself."

"Commissioner," Shane answers with a slight nod.

Elsa walks Cliff down the hallway, gives his shoulder a squeeze and closes the door after him. When Shane brings his tea and a few cookies upstairs just minutes later, she shuts off the kitchen lights.

Well, she thinks. That's that, then. Off Shane will go, and they all made it through the night. Somehow, someway. Everyone can take a deep breath now and start fresh. She looks out that same window where moonlight falls on the inn's rolling lawn, on the ornamental dune grasses and now-empty bistro table. And that's where she pauses, holding back the white curtain and gazing toward the distant beach.

"Soon the sun will rise," she whispers with a glance to the sky. "Ocean stars will shine and the tide will turn … as it always does."

twenty-one

3:00 a.m. – Sunday

THE QUIETNESS HERE AT THE lake is different. It's not like at home, on the bay. Kyle stands in the cabin's bathroom and drags a hand down his cheek. The window is open, and he's aware of the woods outside. And the small, glassy lake. Beneath the moonlight, the water looks like a silver painting fringed with sweeping wild grasses. Around it, trees rise in shadow against the night sky.

But it's the sounds of the woods that he notices. The earlier chorus of crickets and katydids has slowed, as though they're turning in now, too. But in the lull, instead of hearing gentle waves breaking on the bay, he hears the hoot of an owl, silence, then another round of *hoot-hoot, hoot-hoot-hoot*. Something about that throaty call is dark itself, coming from the tall pine trees outside the cabin window.

It's silent on the other side of the door, too. Lauren's waiting out there for him. She's been quiet since she got here. Their words have been cautious, but sparse. Sometimes, even awkward. Which Kyle totally gets, especially when he thinks of the angry words he spewed that afternoon, in their bedroom at Stony Point. Words about not being able to stand beside her on the beach and renew their commitment to each other.

Still, tonight Lauren let that go and tried again to explain *why* she did what she did. Why she sent his estranged brother an invitation to their vow renewal ceremony.

"Don't you remember what Sal said about second chances?" she asked, her head tipped, her chignon barely holding on, her eyes nearly defeated.

"*Molto speciale.*" As he said it, Kyle's voice broke. That's how close to the end of his rope he'd gotten.

Lauren nodded. "*Very special,*" she whispered. "I wanted that for *you*. That very special reconciliation with someone you once loved." She fought her own emotion before saying, "That's what the day was about, Kyle. Love."

Kyle shakes his head now, turns on the faucet, bends and splashes cold water on his face for a good, long minute. But nothing will wash away the shame he feels for his behavior. After patting his face and neck dry, he tightens the drawstring on his green-plaid pajama bottoms and puts on a clean tee. He gives another quick look in the mirror before opening the door to find Lauren sitting at the dining room table. The birch-bark lampshades on the chandelier glow softly; a basket centerpiece spills over with pinecones. To the side, a pail also wrapped in birch bark, and filled with tall purple lavender stems, sits beside a flickering lantern on the hearth. Kyle takes a deep breath, then presses that damp towel along his hairline before doing anything else. He knows this is all on him to fix.

"Thanks for bringing me a change of clothes," he calls out as he rehangs the damp towel. "I wasn't thinking straight before and didn't pack anything." He shuts off the bathroom light, walks across the living room and sits beside Lauren at the table. "I thought I'd just drive here to do some thinking."

Lauren reaches over and simply squeezes his hand, then slides his cup of tea closer. "You look tired. We can talk more tomorrow?"

"No. Well, yes. But I want to tell you something." Kyle looks at her. She's changed into her nightclothes—navy satin sleepshirt and light robe. A small stone pendant hangs from a gold chain on her neck. But it's her hair that gets to him. Her sad chignon that she twisted up hours ago with such high hopes is long gone, her blonde hair brushed out now. He reaches up and touches a soft strand. "Funny thing about today is, I never said anything … but Shane's been on my mind. On and off, the past year."

Lauren cups her tea close, only listening.

"You know," Kyle continues, "the very first time I ever lit a church candle, it was at my father's funeral." He leans his arms on the table and takes a long breath. "Fifteen years ago now. But the candle wasn't for Dad. Even then, it was for Shane. As mad as I was at the time, I lit it for him. And since then, I've occasionally stopped in at St. Bernard's Church and lit more candles for him. Don't know why. He was just on my mind. This past year, even more so. At Aria's baptism a few weeks ago, I did it again."

Lauren sips her tea, then drags her fingers across his arm. Kyle's not sure if she's going to say something, or if she's just there for him. So he waits, too.

"Maybe," she says so softly, he has to tip his head to hear her words, "your conscience was telling you something. Telling you to face something bothering you? Because, come on ..." She turns to him and touches his face, then folds her hands around her cup again. "You think of life differently by the water. And since we've moved to our house on the bay, the sea's just across the street. How can you *not* think of your childhood summers with your brother, when you spent them at that very beach?"

"Exactly. But it was always just thoughts in my head. Memories. And I was good with that. Then, when Elsa told me Shane was actually *at* the inn, I couldn't face the reality of his presence." His voice drops then. "God, Ell. I'm so sorry, because you caught the brunt of it. And I hurt you." Kyle slowly turns his teacup, waiting. Hoping Lauren will say the right words.

But she doesn't. She's as quiet as he is. Instead, Kyle hears that owl call again, a little further out in the woods this time.

"I'm *really* sorry for overreacting," Kyle admits, "is what I'm trying to say."

And putting that into words mortifies him. He drops his head with regret. Closes his eyes against the vision of him storming into their bedroom when Lauren was wearing her absolutely gorgeous wedding dress.

"Some things?" she begins, her voice low. "Some things you can never be prepared for, Kyle."

As she says it, her voice is as distant as that owl's now. And as dark. Lauren's thoughts have gone elsewhere, and Kyle knows. His wife's had her own run-ins with being unprepared. Run-ins that knocked her right off her feet. It's apparent as she shrugs and gives him a sad smile.

Her look says it all.

Says she's expert on being unprepared. Knows all about not being prepared to leave Kyle for another man—for Neil Barlow—ten years ago, days before Neil died; wasn't prepared for Kyle getting his diamond ring back on her finger and marrying her, regardless; was not only unprepared, but ambushed by the fact that Evan, who she was pregnant with when they got married, was actually Neil's son.

If anyone knows about being unprepared, Kyle thinks as he sips his tea, it's Lauren. Yet she soldiers on.

"Do you think you'll talk to Shane?" she asks. "He is at the inn, after all."

Kyle takes his teacup to the window and looks out at the night. Night *here*, he thinks. Night at Stony Point. One thing's for certain, no matter where. It's a night that seems endless.

"Tomorrow?" Lauren persists from the table. "Before he leaves?"

"I don't know." Kyle tips back the last of his tea, turns and takes her cup, too. "Maybe," he says on his way to the kitchen sink.

Problem then is that Kyle can't get the thought out of his head.

The thought of coming face-to-face with his long-lost brother.

The one he'd written off as dead fifteen years ago, sitting around a bonfire at Little Beach.

As Kyle turns off the lights in their little cabin; as he straightens a hooked pillow on the couch, then extinguishes the lantern flame on the hearth; as Lauren folds down the patchwork coverlet on their bed, then turns to gaze at the lake outside beneath the moonlight, Kyle only pictures being in the same room as Shane. Speaking difficult words. Words he'd sometimes rather choke on than say. Words and looks he'd rather leave alone.

Even as he gets into bed—the mattress creaking beneath him, the blanket light on his skin—the thought is there. Beneath the ruffled curtain topper, moonlight throws very little light into the dark room. But it's enough to make out faint details. So Kyle looks at the ceiling, unable to even close his eyes. When he tries, all he imagines is some pained reconciliation with his brother. So instead, he keeps himself awake, listening for that owl. With a glance toward the paned bedside window, maybe he's just waiting for the first rays of sun. For another day to take over.

At least until Lauren drops her robe on the foot of the bed and lies beside him in the darkness. Wearing her cool satin nightshirt, she settles on her side, facing him. And Kyle believes she falls asleep in the few silent minutes of time that pass, until she moves a little closer.

"Can I ask you something?" she whispers.

"Always. You can always ask me *anything*." Kyle turns his face toward her and can just about make out her grey eyes watching him. Her lightly freckled nose, sun-kissed before their vow renewal. Her long blonde hair—so mussed, and beautiful—against her navy nightshirt. "What is it?" he whispers back. Because after the past godawful day, what else can either of them do but whisper?

But try.

But fight back a sob and force a few kind words.

But grasp onto any look, any touch, and cling to it.

"Would you just hold me?" Lauren asks.

Wordlessly, Kyle does. But when he shifts closer and slips one arm beneath her shoulders, the other across her waist, he can't miss the way she closes her eyes against tears. Which just about breaks his heart in two. So he presses a kiss to the side of her head, feeling her soft hair beneath his lips. They are still then, with only that moonlight shining outside. All's quiet at the lake. There are no lapping waves, like on the bay.

Just stillness. Just peace.

Minutes pass. Enough time ticks by when he's not sure if she's fallen asleep or not. But her breathing is regular. Her body relaxed.

"No matter what, Ell," Kyle barely whispers. "I'm never letting go."

twenty-two

3:45 a.m. – Sunday

MARIS LIES ON THE COUCH. Through the open porch windows, warm air drifts in. It touches her skin as lightly as he does. With her eyes closed in the darkness, it's hard to decipher the two: summer breeze, or Shane's touch. He runs his fingers along the skin of her arm, up to her shoulder, her neck. There, he tips her face toward his.

Still, her eyes are closed. But her lips smile, especially when she feels his lips there, too. Pressing against her mouth as his hand moves behind her neck and tugs up through her hair.

"I can't stay," she whispers into his kiss, but does nothing to stop it.

"Yes, you can. For a little while," he whispers back. He strokes her hair fanned across the sofa pillow.

Being on the enclosed porch on this hot summer night, it almost feels as though they are outdoors. Outside sounds are close. A breeze rustles tree leaves. Crickets chirp. A lone car drives past the house.

And that air coming through all those open porch windows? As sweet as his touch. But making it hard for her to pull herself away from the porch, from the couch.

From Shane.

She takes one of his hands, drags her fingers along the open palm and feels the work it does. Feels the salty rope uncoiling beneath it. Feels the heavy lobster traps pulled dripping from the ocean. Feels the wet lobsters measured before being tossed in the tank or back to sea. Feels the stuffed netted bait bags loaded into those lobster traps.

"Stay." Shane takes *her* hand then and feels every bend, every finger, the curve of her wrist.

"But it's getting late."

"God, I've missed you."

"You're just saying that." Maris leaves a kiss on his jaw, his neck.

"But I never forget how gorgeous you are." As he tells her, his fingers toy with her hair. He slides them over thick strands left wavy after he unwound her French braid earlier. Kisses her, too. Her forehead. Her mouth. When his hand moves to her tank-top blouse and slips aside the fabric on her shoulder, he kisses her there, then, too.

"I *really* have to go," Maris tells him again, this time half sitting and straightening her top.

"Okay. After one more kiss."

In the darkness, she looks at him lying beside her on the sofa. She drags her fingers through his hair, coarse with salt.

And she sinks down lower for that one last kiss.

"*Come here, Mare*," Shane whispers, as if she can get any closer to him. Their bodies already press together on the couch. But she tries, and shifts in his hold. When she does, his two hands cradle her face, his eyes looking at hers.

"Only *one* kiss," she reminds him, gently touching a finger to his lips.

After a moment, he only nods. Nods, and leans in to press his mouth to hers. That's not all, though. His hands, they reach around her neck and tangle in her hair.

There's something about the summer night, and something about this being the last kiss of it, that strikes Maris. Oh, there's no denying that neither of them wants this kiss to end. But Shane especially doesn't. Not when he deepens that kiss in a way that has her open her mouth to his. And his hands, they don't let go. Instead, like a wave, they wash over her. One behind her back now, low, holding her close.

And still, they kiss. One kiss.

They're quiet, though. Because they're not alone in the house and have to be careful. So the only noise is their breathing, and her soft moan, and his hand pressing back her hair as he moves half on top of her. She feels the length of his body against hers.

Feels that one kiss, still unbroken.

A kiss that has turned into more now. More, as his hand moves along the tiny buttons of her silky tank-top blouse. The blouse she'd put back on and buttoned up once already after they'd quickly slept together in his pickup truck.

But that kiss? His lips don't leave hers as his fingers only undo the top blouse buttons this time, his hand skimming her breasts, her skin, as he does.

And that kiss ... Still happening as he slips her partially buttoned blouse off one shoulder. She feels his hand slip down a bra strap, too, then move beneath her black bra, over her breasts, before sliding down her side beneath her tangled-up blouse.

One kiss? She's not sure she's ever had a more intimate one. It's all she can do to not catch her breath, to murmur his name. But she doesn't dare break the kiss. One that instead has her hand move beneath his tee, across his chest, and down his belly. One that has her next pulling the light blanket off the back of the couch to somewhat cover up before reaching beneath it and unbuckling his leather belt again. Unzipping his jeans.

Which has him do the same. After getting his fingers out of her half off blouse, his hands brusquely lower her frayed denim shorts, her panties. She pulls up her leg as he presses the clothes off them, their bodies twisting together.

But that kiss? Still going on, going down.

It's a kiss Maris never saw coming, and the likes of one she's never had before. Somehow, Shane gave her one kiss, just *one*, and it's lasting the entire time they get out of just enough clothes to do it again. The entire time he moves on top of her and her legs straddle him.

One kiss as they have sex, silently, moving beneath that blanket as his hand slips behind her back and pulls her close, their skin moist with perspiration, his mouth ever on hers.

When the kiss is nearly done, Maris feels it. Feels the end begin as Shane touches her damp hair, her flushed face, turning that one long kiss into several smaller, reluctant ones. When it finally does end, when Shane shifts off of her and says in her ear, "*One kiss, Mare,*" Maris bolts up, her hand to her heart with the surprise of what just happened, her breath coming in a shuddering gasp.

"Maris?"

"What?" She whips around in the darkness, her hand trying to cover up and straighten her tangled blouse. "Oh! Oh, *Jason,*" she whispers loudly as she sinks back down into the bed.

"What's the matter?" Jason's voice comes to her. "You jumped."

Maris lies there staring at the ceiling, then looks toward the open window, open enough for the warm night air to drop down on her. Just like that night with Shane. "I jumped?"

"Yes."

"What do you mean?" Maris asks, all while wondering if Jason can tell she's seriously trying to slow her panicked heart.

"You startled. And gasped."

"Oh."

Nothing then, just a pause before Jason continues. "Bad dream?"

Dream. Oh, *that* was no dream, Maris thinks. That night with Shane happened, and is as clear as if it happened just minutes ago—not *years* ago, on the same day that she finished stitching those stars at the dock. That evening, after fooling around in Shane's parked pickup, they ended up at his house in Eastfield for a few hours. They'd hung out on the enclosed porch because his father was inside watching TV before he went upstairs to bed. But she and Shane stayed on the porch where the air was cooler. The darkness inviting. Their touches stolen. She's never forgotten how, when Shane had whispered, *One more kiss*, he drew that kiss out to the longest she's ever had—before or since. No kiss has ever come close. Not even with Jason.

No, that was no dream. That memory was as vivid as living the moment.

"A bad dream?" Maris asks. "No. Your snoring woke me." In the silence then, she reaches to Jason's side of the bed to pat his arm.

"Over here, sweetheart," Jason says as he switches on a bedside lamp.

Maris half sits up, blinks against the light and looks over at him sitting in his chair. He's still wearing his suit pants, with his dress shirt loose beneath the unbuttoned vest. His forearm crutches lean against the chair.

"I just got home, darling. Haven't even gotten my leg off yet, never mind been to sleep. Just got back from that cabin in Addison."

"That's *right*," she says with a sleepy shake of her head. "How'd it go?"

"Lauren's there. I brought her to see Kyle."

"Oh, good!" Propped up on her elbows, Maris watches Jason as he takes off a shoe. "Is Shane still here? At the inn?"

"Don't know," Jason tells her while setting down the shoe. "But I hope not. Cliff was supposed to evict him." Jason rolls up his left pant leg. "Everything okay here with you?"

"With me? Yeah." Lightly rubbing her forehead, she says, "Might've had a little too much wine with my sister."

"Get some rest. You'll feel better in the morning."

"Yeah, maybe."

"*You* haven't seen Shane around, have you?" Jason asks while removing his prosthetic leg. "You and Eva?"

"No."

Not in reality, anyway, she thinks while sinking back down in the bed. The last thing she and Jason need to do is start discussing Shane Bradford, in reality *or* dreams. One misstep, one wrong word and Jason will be onto her like a hawk—yep, talons open and ready to ensnare her. So it's best to change the subject.

"What time is it?" she asks.

"Late. Three forty-five. Go back to sleep."

Straightening her black satin pajama top, Maris sits up again. When Jason sets his prosthesis aside and looks at her, she tells him, "I need something to drink."

It isn't until she's in the bathroom, though, that she lets out a long breath, first. Then she closes her eyes and splashes cold water on her face. Even once the tap's off, she stays bent over the sink, hands over her face for several moments before blindly reaching for a towel and drying off. The bathroom window is open, too, letting the damp air into the room. After hanging the towel, Maris glances out that window to the sky. Funny how there's already a change in its color—it's paler now that it's almost four in the morning. Time's moved, the tides have shifted, the sun's ready to rise on a new day. All that apparent in a change of the night's hue.

Before returning to bed, and to Jason, Maris sits on the edge of the bathtub. Just sits there, feels the cool tile beneath her bare feet, and breathes.

Then breathes again.

twenty-three

7:00 a.m. – Sunday

SHANE WAS GOOD FOR HIS word.

Elsa's not surprised when she goes upstairs and turns into his room on Sunday morning. Still in her turquoise caftan, she stops in the doorway. The window blinds are open, and early sunbeams shine on the hardwood floor, the distressed-white shiplap walls. Everything is in its place, neat as a pin. The bed has been stripped and made, the linens folded on a nearby chair. A checked quilt left at the foot of a sea-green bedspread. Elsa walks into the room and opens the drawers of the white-painted dresser. Each drawer, empty. She looks to the left. The beadboard closet door is ajar, so she ventures over. It's empty, too. No button-down shirts on a hanger; no newsboy cap on a hook; no duffel on the shelf. So she turns around and scans the room. Everything—from the small desk beneath a window to the shelves on the boardwalk-planked accent wall—looks as if no one had even stayed here.

Except for that desk, which catches her eye. Its drawer is not quite closed, and she notices the open box of vintage stationery. She and Celia had scoured tag sales and antique shops for enough old stationery to stock a small supply in each guest's room. Some of the stationery has seashell borders; some scrollwork in the corners; some are scenic fold-it postalette cards with wishing well or lighthouse images. Lined or blank, watercolored or stamped, a woman might want to send a seaside message to a friend while sitting at a window table overlooking the Sound. Or maybe a man would jot a few affectionate lines to someone he thinks of while staying at the beach inn. Or a couple could pen a special memory, roll it up with a piece of twine and drop it in their courtesy happiness jar.

So Elsa picks up the box and quietly thumbs through the envelopes, counting quietly. "One, two, three, four." She tips her head and counts again. Yes. Four envelopes, when she knows each room had been stacked with five. Once more, she lifts the envelope corners. "One, two, three, *four*." Still holding the box, she looks in the wicker wastebasket to see if maybe one envelope got tossed. If maybe Shane started writing something, then changed his mind.

Nothing's there. The wastebasket's empty. So someone, somewhere, will receive a message on her Ocean Star Inn vintage stationery. Shane sat at this very table and put pen to paper, for someone. Elsa looks around. But that's it. Other than a missing envelope, there's no evidence he'd even been here.

"Wait," she whispers. There. He forgot something. His happiness jar is on the bedside table. So Elsa picks up the Mason jar, looks at the fine sand and few seashells in it, then holds it close. He added nothing of his own. No keepsake of some memory from his brief stay at her inn. No trinket from his late-night beach walk. No memento of happiness.

No, Shane Bradford just came in alone and then receded like the tide. Just like that.

But what's surprising in the Sunday morning quiet is that Elsa's actually sad.

Because yesterday came and went, too. The day had started with such hopeful expectations, and quickly changed into something much darker. The thing is, when it *was* here, the day—good or bad—was eternal. It seemed like it would just never come to an end.

Now? Now in the silent inn, Elsa feels the void of Shane's absence. She goes to his window and straightens a thin white starfish propped there, then looks out toward the distant beach. All evidence of the failed vow renewal ceremony is gone. All the décor collected and stored away. The folding white chairs stacked and awaiting pickup. Giving a sad shake of her head, Elsa thinks of Kyle and Lauren. Of their big day that evaporated like the sea mist.

Most sad, though, is that there had been no reconciliation between two brothers, either. Not a few words said. Not a reluctant hug. Nothing to bridge some painful, difficult gap between them.

Elsa turns then and walks out of the room. Worst of all,

there was not even a goodbye between Shane and Kyle. It was all for naught, every bit of the day. If there had been at *least* some words between them, it might have made the cancelled vow renewal ceremony less painful.

When Elsa gets to the kitchen, she sets Shane's happiness jar on the counter. He seemed taken with the idea of her jars, so she's surprised he left his behind. Shane also rinsed his teacup and saucer; both are in the dish rack. When she opens the window over her sink, fresh sea air wafts in. Oh, who can help but breathe in deeply at the first scent of that salt from the sea …

So she does, breathing in once, then again. *Cures what ails you*, she sadly thinks. If only, especially today. So many of them need a little tonic to ease their lives this morning, of that she can be sure.

Because today should have been a happy day, too. One filled with sweet memories, with recalled visions of the bride and groom waltzing on the sand; of Celia strumming her guitar; of Jason and Maris, Eva, Matt, everybody, sitting at tables with good food and drink; of lingering together over dessert in the original Foley's back room, jukebox songs floating on that salt air. Today should have been spent looking at photographs on cell phones and smiling at the moments. Elsa's own phone should be ringing with calls that can't contain their happiness from the wonderful event at her Ocean Star Inn.

But when Elsa turns around to the empty kitchen, the room is pin-drop quiet, instead. Which is exactly like it was after Sal died last summer.

When she'd wake up and walk alone through her empty cottage, stand in Sal's bedroom, then come to the kitchen.

Today, it's like nothing's changed. She's doing it all over again.

"We'll all get past this, too. Somehow," she whispers as she opens the refrigerator spilling with uneaten vow-renewal food that will go to such waste.

"Unless …" she says, tapping a finger to her lips and surveying the wrapped-and-covered dishes stuffed every which way on each refrigerated shelf. "*Unless.*"

She goes to her marble-top island and puts on her leopard-print reading glasses. Her cell phone is also there, plugged in to charge for the new day. "Well," Elsa tells herself, "it *better* be good and charged, for the responses it's about to receive."

With that, she sits on a stool and sets up a group text message on her phone.

Buongiorno, she types. *I hope you're all rested and the new day brings clear thoughts. A note, this morning, to let you know that Shane has packed and left the inn. He's gone, and now we all need to talk and to calm down. So…*

Please Come: Sunday Dinner
When: Today, August 14, 4 PM
Where: Ocean Star Inn
Attire: Casual
Bring: Good Vibes Only

twenty-four

7:20 a.m. – Sunday

PARADISE IS OPEN TO INTERPRETATION, and this is Jason's.

Maris knows it. They all do, for that matter. Jason's said it often enough in heated debates of their age-old question: *What's your definition of paradise?* Said it while Nick argued the merits of a deluxe, sauce-dripping cheeseburger at The Sand Bar; or while Kyle defined paradise as the time spent standing behind the big stoves at his diner. Jason always politely acknowledges everyone else's paradise, like Matt's description of cruising the highways in a rented RV. But Jason's sure to point out that no one's paradise is the be-all, get-all. Which might get the gang to hoot and argue, to defend their own personal definitions.

But Jason persists. "Paradise is open to interpretation," he'll say. And when everyone from Nick to Cliff to Elsa to Vinny asks him what his paradise could *possibly* be, he goes quiet for a minute, then reveals it. "Sunday mornings in bed with my wife."

And oh, doesn't Maris know it. The way he lounges beneath the sheet, eyes closed, breathing the warm salt air drifting in the windows, listening to the seagulls crying out on the bluff ... She can just visualize Jason in his paradise, lying there with his arm flung over his eyes, utterly relaxed after making love with her. Until his slow grin comes when she moves to do it again.

There's no denying it. Maris would've been the first to insist it's the truth. Would've sworn that Jason's paradise will always be lying in bed with her on Sunday mornings.

But not today.

This Sunday morning, she looks closely at him. Her husband is so gone. He's in the throes of deep sleep, the likes of which she hasn't seen before. His sheer exhaustion is apparent. He hasn't moved at all in hours. Beyond the bed, his vow renewal clothes are tossed across his chair.

She watches him longer, then touches his face. His arm.

Nothing. He doesn't wake up. It is so obvious how depleted he is after everything he did for everybody else yesterday.

For Kyle, trying to calm down the groom. To get him to clear his thoughts. To breathe.

For Lauren, so devastated at the turn of events. Jason couldn't do enough to comfort her, to get her to the cabin in Addison. To talk her through her worries.

For Cliff, even. Jason made sure that the beach Cliff patrols was stripped clean of all vow renewal décor. This way, vacationers' seaside Sunday wouldn't be marred by the sight of unused chairs and tiki torches. By the sight of something gone so wrong.

Looking at Jason's whiskered face; at his hair wavy in the August humidity; at his slow, even breathing, what Maris knows is this: If you're on the list of people Jason Barlow cares about, he'll always buoy you up. He did so for Kyle and Lauren all day yesterday. And today, Maris loves him even more for it.

When Jason's cell phone dings on the nightstand, she quietly reaches for it, shuts off the sound and lies back down. Holding the phone close, she reads a text message from Elsa. Reads it once, then once again.

"*Oh, thank God,*" she whispers.

Jason felt her. Felt Maris' touch on his face, along the hairs of his arm. And it was exquisite, that feather touch. A touch enough for him to be aware of it, but not enough to wake him, to get him out of his slumber. If anything, her touch got him to breathe even deeper, to rest more. It relaxed him that much.

No, it was the simple ding of his cell phone that did it— that pulled him from his sleep. One dinging sound and he knew the world around him was up and at 'em. And now they'd be up and at *him*. So when Maris reaches over for the phone, he opens his eyes and watches her settle back down on her pillow, phone in hand. She wears that black satin short set he likes, and her beautiful hair is sleep-mussed. Really, he only wants to reach out and stroke it.

But instead, he watches her intently reading some early-morning text message. God knows it must be filled with the latest news, the Stony Point headline of the hour. His wife squints and slowly scrolls down the text.

"*Oh, thank God*," Maris whispers, still reading.

Jason watches her a moment longer. "What is it?" he finally asks. When she startles at the sound of his voice, he tips his head, still watching her.

"Jason! I thought you were sleeping."

"I'm up now." He reaches over to touch a long strand of her brown hair. "So who *else* is awake and texting at this hour on a Sunday morning?"

"It's Elsa. She sent a group text letting us all know that Shane left. Apparently he packed his bags overnight and is gone now."

Jason turns over and lies on his back, absentmindedly scratching his chest. "How do you like that? Cliff did it, then."

"Did what?"

"I was tied up last night with Kyle, over at Mitch's place and at that cabin in the woods. There was no time to talk to Shane to see if I could get him to leave. So I asked Cliff to do it."

"Cliff? And he agreed?"

Jason shrugs. "I said all he'd have to do is throw his commissioner weight around to get Shane on his way. Must've worked. The Judge came through."

Maris lifts the phone and reads the screen again. "There's more," she says, her voice hushed. "Now that Shane's gone, Elsa's having Sunday dinner at the inn. She wants to talk with everybody to be sure we're all okay." Maris glances over when Jason holds out his open hand. "Which is really sweet. Think Lauren and Kyle will show up?" she asks, dropping the phone in Jason's palm.

He takes the phone and reads Elsa's message. "Don't know."

"Well, I'll go make us coffee and bring it up," Maris says while tossing back the sheets and getting out of bed.

"Okay, good."

"You're tired." She leaves a soft trail of kisses on his face, neck and shoulder, then gently removes the phone from his hand. "Stay in bed and rest."

Jason turns his head and watches her cross the room to the doorway, then flings his arm over his eyes. "Yesterday was one helluva day," he says to no one but himself.

⁓

Kyle half dozes in bed, lulled by the woodsy sounds. Heck, waking up here in a Connecticut country cabin, you'd think you were in an animated nature movie. Outside there'd be gentle animals all wide-eyed and inquisitive. The happy birds would drape garlands of berries from one tree to another as their twittering songs filled the air. Pretty deer might stand in lush flowerbeds while fairy dust glittered in the sunbeams.

Kyle keeps his eyes closed as warm air drops through the window like a light blanket on his skin. Listening to chirping and peeping chickadees and cardinals and robins outside, he figures you might as well cue the sweeping violins as fish no doubt fly from the silvery lake.

Until his cell phone dings. Kyle reaches for it, then forces his eyes open to read the message.

"Ell." He gently nudges his, well okay, his sleeping beauty. Her blonde hair is fanned on the pillow, her skin golden, the eyelashes of her closed eyes brushing her face. "Wake up, Ell."

Lauren merely sighs, then pulls the sheet up higher.

Still, there's something about the text message that has Kyle reading it again. He props his pillow behind him and sits up against the headboard, looks at the phone, then at Lauren. And what he sees is this: Lauren is still in that peaceful, slumbering moment when yesterday hasn't caught up to her waking yet. There's no stress on her face, no tension in her body.

"I can't believe this," Kyle quietly says, getting back to the text. He drags a hand through his hair. "No way. Shane actually left Stony Point."

"What?" Lauren asks without moving. Without lifting open an eyelid.

"According to Elsa." Kyle lowers the phone and looks toward that window with those twittering, happy birds on the other side of it. "And here I was ready to talk and confront him. You know, mental preparation is half the battle, and I did it. I prepared mentally. That's what most of yesterday was all about for me. I prepared in my head to responsibly face the brother I'd evicted from my life. And now?" He raises the phone again and reads the text message. "Now he's gone. *Gone*. I'm sure he already got himself on some lobster boat and has left land far behind."

"Gone for good, you think?"

"Looks it. So that's that." Problem is, as he says it, Kyle feels oddly disappointed. Oddly ... defeated. Those birds sing a little softer, with some wistfulness in their song now.

"Let me see." Lauren reaches over and takes the phone from him. "Oh, no."

"What?"

"Did you keep reading? Elsa wants us all at the inn for Sunday dinner."

"Shit."

"To talk." Lauren hands him the phone back. "Want to skip it?"

"No." He reads the rest of Elsa's message. "I'd *like* to skip it, but no. Everyone was so shocked yesterday, when we cancelled the ceremony. So Elsa's dinner could be our chance to explain things—and apologize. Heck, this way, we'll only have to do it one time, if we catch everybody there around her big dining room table."

"Go without me?"

"What?"

"Go without me." Lauren props herself up on her elbows and looks around the bedroom. "I saw everyone yesterday and just cannot rehash things." Slowly, she sinks back down on the bed and fluffs the pillow behind her head. "It's too much for me to go through that again."

Kyle lies down on his side and touches her hair. "I'll stay here with you, then."

"No. Going and seeing everyone is the right thing to do. But I need *you* to do it today. And don't stay too long at Elsa's?"

"Okay." Kyle draws a finger from her shoulder down to her wrist. "Okay. I'll try to clear the air, have a bite to eat and come back here."

"Then what? Maybe we'll pick up the kids at my parents'?"

"No." Now Kyle gets out of bed and walks to the window. Outside, sunshine glints off the lake, where wisps of mist rise. "Because I was thinking, Ell. We can *stay* here." Kyle turns and looks at the bedroom with its wood-planked walls. Rough-hewn beams crisscross the ceiling; the patchwork quilt is folded on the end of the bed; a collection of decorative wooden birdhouses lines a wall shelf; a fishing pole leans in the corner.

"*Stay* here?" Again Lauren props herself up. "Really?"

"Sure. The cabin's rented. We paid for it, after all. You can check in with your parents, who were going to watch the kids anyway. And Jerry's covering the diner."

"I don't know. Evan and Hailey have to be so upset at what happened yesterday."

Kyle looks at Lauren. "We'll call them today. And we'll see them when we get back, don't worry. But we have to talk still, you and me. So we'll do that, here. And … and, we'll unplug, too. Yeah." Kyle remembers what Mitch told him about Thoreau's solitary gig in the woods. "Yeah, we'll unplug from everyone, from *everything*. Just tell your parents to use the cabin phone to reach us. Because, Ell?" Kyle sits on the edge of the bed, touches her face and takes a long breath. "We need to get back to where we were. Just the two of us. Things were going so good. I mean, we're living at the beach, money's all right, we were happy and getting by. You were painting more and more. Let's do it, here. Get back to all that, now that my brother's gone."

"I'm not sure, Kyle. Maybe what we need to get back to is real life. Close up the cabin and put this weekend behind us."

Kyle goes to that paned window again. If he's not mistaken, he can smell the scent of the pines from here. "No. No, because Mitch told me that Thoreau worked out his thoughts in a cabin in the woods." He looks over his shoulder at Lauren, still in bed. "I know we've only got a few days. But maybe we can, too."

∽

A warbled ding sound wakes up Cliff. He reaches over from his futon and checks his cell phone. Nothing. The problem with living, illegally or not, in this beach association's metal trailer is that the metal walls sometimes block his cell phone service.

So he lies there beneath a light blanket for a few more minutes, waiting to see if another ding will sound. Or if some early Sunday morning text message will make its way to his phone screen. A framed seascape painting hangs beside the futon, and he looks at it. In the painting, seagulls soar over waves breaking on a rocky ledge on the coast. There's a lighthouse, too, rising from the rocks. His trailer is so far from the bluff, and the beach, he never hears the waves break, the seagulls cry. So he likes to look at this painting and at least imagine those coastal sounds.

Except today, he's imagining what desperate text message is headed his way—if only he had cell service. So he sits up, steps into his slippers, puts on his navy robe and walks around the trailer while holding the phone high above his head.

"Nothing," he mutters when he checks the screen. Nothing more than a spinning signal-symbol as the phone hunts for a meager bar of service. He heads to the window to try there, and notices a different signal when he looks outside.

The red flag is flipped up on his mailbox.

"I'll be darned," Cliff whispers. "Shane did it," he tells himself while heading to the door. "Crossed his t's, dotted his i's and is good for his word."

After opening the steel entry door and stepping outside, Cliff first drops his phone in his robe pocket, then looks both ways before hurrying to the mailbox. There, he pulls out a sealed envelope. It's vintage-looking. Cream-colored, with a sketched starfish embossed on the back flap. But it's the front side that Cliff runs his hand over. Written in strong cursive is one word: *Lauren*. As Cliff gives it a look, then glances down the street as though he might see Shane's pickup leaving—taking the curve toward the stone trestle—his cell phone dings again. Clearly, this time. He pulls the phone from his robe pocket, then tosses one more glance toward the trestle. And sees nothing.

Finally—with Shane's letter in one hand, cell phone in the other—Cliff sits outside on the top metal step of his industrial trailer-home and reads Elsa's Sunday dinner invitation. As he's reading, more dings come. It's the kids all instantly replying to Elsa. Thumbs-up emoji from Nick; *Will love to see everyone together* from Paige and Vinny; Eva offers to *Bring a side dish*. Jason and Maris send a simple *We'll be there*. Nothing yet from Kyle and Lauren.

So Cliff rereads Elsa's invitation and types in *Affirmative*.

Instead of going inside and putting on the coffee then, maybe scrambling an egg or two on his hot plate, Cliff just sits there in the sunshine. Sits in his robe on the metal trailer step and leans to the side, hoping for some glance of a departing Shane Bradford.

Because Cliff oddly feels the weight of Shane's glaring absence on the texted invite list.

Feels the weight of matters in Lauren's sealed letter, too.

So for a few minutes, he just sits there in the sun, feeling a little disappointed.

And with good reason. The letter, the Sunday dinner, the exclusion of Shane from Stony Point, well ... something about it all just doesn't feel right.

twenty-five

4:40 p.m. – Sunday

Now THIS IS SOMETHING JASON wouldn't mind resuming in his life: Sunday dinners at Elsa's. Over the past year, the Meet and Eats the gang had initiated to stay close after Sal's death often ended up here at the inn. Which suited Elsa just fine. She made no bones about declaring them all her official taste-testers as she perfected future inn recipes.

Sunday dinners will be included for all my guests once the Ocean Star Inn opens, she would explain.

And Jason relished being a taste-tester. Eating Elsa's home-cooked meals during the past year had been a highlight of his week. Skillet steak with mushrooms; roasted chicken and scalloped potatoes; Bolognese stuffed peppers; barbecued pork chops. All with sides of oven-roasted broccoli or Parmesan-herb sweet potatoes, topped off with sea-salted, caramel-swirled brownies or some such decadent dessert. Actually, he's not sure he's ever been so well fed. But during these past couple of months, Elsa's gotten busy with her new granddaughter, and with final preparations for the inn's September opening. So busy that her exalted Sunday dinners have fallen by the wayside.

Until today.

All it took was one emotional upheaval to prompt Elsa to pull everyone back together, seated at her grand dining room table: he and Maris; his sister, Paige, and brother-in-law, Vinny; Matt and Eva; Celia; Cliff and Nick; Kyle. Before them, a full spread of vow-renewal leftovers—mini meatballs and stuffed mushrooms; salads and warm crusty bread; lasagna and chicken parm—is heated and set on antique china platters. Crystal goblets and linen napkins anchor each place setting; sun-bleached seashells lean against flickering silver lanterns on both ends of the long, wood-planked table. Each distressed-navy, French country chair is filled; serving utensils scoop heaping, cheesy portions; voices murmur and talk around the table.

But when a silver knife is tapped on a crystal glass, the clinking sound rings through the air. Still chatting, everyone turns to Kyle, who is standing while clinking that glass. Not surprising, he looks tired. The emotion of the weekend shows on his face. As he taps the glass, everyone slowly stops talking. It isn't until the room goes silent that Kyle sets down his knife and looks first to Elsa at the head of the table. She's dressed casual today, wearing a long black sleeveless blouse over white skinny pants, a heavy gold bracelet on her wrist.

"Elsa," Kyle begins. "Let me start by thanking you for inviting us all here to dinner. I wish Lauren could've made it, too, but she's taking a breather after yesterday's, well, craziness. And you can figure that yesterday is why I'm here now."

"I'm happy to do this, Kyle," Elsa assures him. "I think everybody can use a nice hot meal and get settled down a little."

"Which is what me and Lauren will do *after* this here dinner. We're taking a couple of days at that cabin ... unplugged. No text messages, no phone calls, no contact. Lauren's parents are watching the kids, so we're just going to work on getting ourselves grounded again."

"That's good, Kyle. Good!" Eva says. "It's so important to not be distracted and just *be* together." With that, she reaches over and gives Matt's hand a squeeze.

"Hear, hear," Vinny agrees while raising his glass.

"But," Kyle presses on, "you're all our good friends. And we both thought it was important to *first* explain what happened yesterday."

"Would you rather wait until dessert to talk?" Elsa asks. "Sit and enjoy your dinner first?"

"Actually, I'd like to clear the air now. If you don't mind, Elsa. This was really thoughtful of you to invite us all today, and it would be nice if everyone could enjoy these leftovers with no tension. But please, guys. Go ahead and start eating." Kyle sits, too, and looks at each of them around the table. "I'll keep you entertained, at the very least."

"Kyle!" Maris scolds while plucking a stuffed mushroom

from the serving platter. "Don't be so hard on yourself."

"Lord knows you've seen us all in our share of situations," Jason tells him, fork in hand.

"Like you said, we're all *friends*." Maris sets the overloaded mushroom beside a hunk of lasagna on Jason's plate. "We understand that these things happen."

"We *are* friends." Kyle lifts his wineglass and takes a sip. "But today? Today I feel like a stranger here."

"Come on, bro." Jason waves him off while chewing a mouthful of lasagna. "A stranger?"

"Eh. Mostly because I feel incredibly uncomfortable being at this table." Still talking, Kyle spoons a serving of chicken parm and drops it on his plate. "I had really high expectations that yesterday would be a … a *balm*. For all of us, really. I just wanted it to be the day we *all* deserved."

Jason drags a thick slice of bread through tomato sauce on his plate, scooping up dregs of lasagna, too. "But it was *your* day, man. Don't worry about us."

Nick nudges Jason to pass the stuffed mushroom platter. "Yeah, Kyle," Nick adds, spearing two loaded mushrooms topped with breadcrumbs. "You're not responsible for all our angst."

"Angst?" Matt asks. "What kind of angst do you have, Nicholas? Living with your 'rents. Buying that Whaler."

"Fellas," Cliff interrupts from where he sits beside Elsa. "Let Kyle finish. Sounds like he's got something important he wants to get off his chest."

"I do, Judge." Kyle slices his fork through a piece of chicken covered in sauce and melted cheese. "Like I said,

I'd hoped we'd all have a great day, yesterday. But a lot of pressure came with that expectation. My vow renewal was meant to celebrate the ten-year mark of mine and Lauren's marriage. Especially since we had some rocky years there. Didn't even know if we'd make it sometimes. But hell, we all know it's also the ten-year anniversary of *other* things ... Neil's death," Kyle says, nodding to Jason. "And my best man losing his leg."

Jason sits back now. Sits back and stops eating to see just where Kyle's taking this talk. Because suddenly, the table's gotten really quiet as Kyle's words get serious.

"Not to mention," Kyle continues, "it's been one year since Sal left us."

"My sweet son," Elsa murmurs at the end of the table, her eyes filling with tears.

"Right. And a good friend to us all." Kyle looks at her and at Celia—who gives Elsa's hand a squeeze. "So let's face it. Yesterday was going to be a day for the books." He lifts his forkful of chicken parm and holds it aloft. "A new chapter. A new beginning. One after we all made it through some difficult times." Eating his mouthful of food, Kyle waves his fork to signal there's more to say. "Then? Well, then my kid brother showed up. Jesus, it felt like one lousy domino fell and took all the others down with it, just like that. And it's mostly because Shane's *my* brother, and I overreacted—that the day imploded."

Jason leans forward, putting his elbows on the table. "Kyle—"

"No." Kyle cuts him off while standing again, pacing

and holding up his hand. "No, I really feel like I *failed* you guys—the way I maybe wrongly called off the whole day—and I'm sorry. We both are, Lauren and me—"

"Don't apologize," Jason insists, his voice rising, his sharp tone cutting through the room. He hears the anger himself, and is sure the rest of them do, too, when everyone looks at *him* now.

"What?" Kyle asks.

"You heard me." Jason points a rigid finger right at Kyle. "Don't apologize. Because what are you sorry for? That you reacted to a situation?"

Kyle, still standing, simply turns up his hands.

"You had *reason* to react, Kyle. It's all tied in with who you are, and you don't owe us an apology for that. So just sit down. *Now.* Sit and hold on a minute." Jason pulls a hand across his jaw. "Please. And let *me* explain where I'm coming from."

Kyle does, taking his seat and motioning to Jason that he has the floor.

Maris, at the same time, briefly strokes Jason's arm. It's her way, he's sure, of telling him to *watch it*, and go easy on Kyle. So Jason collects his thoughts while holding up his plate for the mini meatballs and slab of chicken parmigiana Maris scooped up for him. Before he eats any of it, though, he looks to Elsa at the end of the table and pauses until she gives him a nod.

So Jason begins.

"My father fought in Vietnam," he says, then lifts the wine bottle and refills his glass. "And before he died a few years back, he liked to tell us—Paige, Neil and me—stories of his time there. I guess after spending those years in the jungles in 'Nam, he was going to make *damn* sure that if nothing else, we would learn *something* about life from it all. And this one day, my brother and I—we were just kids—stayed out later than we should have, traipsing through the marsh. We might've been on the hunt for our version of the VC, which would've been the great egret, standing stock-still in the tall grasses. Or we were doing a sweep along the muddy banks for blue crabs, which for us? Hidden toe-popper mines. We loved doing that, pretending we were soldiers. Neil had on Dad's old boonie hat from the war; I wore my camping vest loaded down with gear. And we waded in the shallows.

"When it got late and we heard a familiar sharp whistle, we knew. Oh, we knew. We were so busted for staying out past curfew. We turned to see Dad at the edge of the marsh, waving us home before the sun set. I can just see him standing there, waiting for us. Neil and I, you can bet we hightailed it to him, but not before tossing our hand-grenade rocks into the marsh, Neil strapping his toy rifle over his shoulder, me finishing the last drops from my canteen.

"Because if my father came *looking* for us, we knew we were in trouble. So that day, we tried apologizing before he could get mad. All breathless, our *I'm sorry ... We were being*

NIGHT BEACH

soldiers in the swamps and *Almost found the enemy ... Sorry, Dad,* did *not* fall on deaf ears. No, it was just the opposite.

"Instead of getting chewed out, we could tell—with relief, I assure you—that he was about to share one of his Vietnam stories." Jason pauses and looks over at his sister, Paige, who is nodding with a small smile. "That evening," Jason continues, "sitting on the banks of the marsh, we heard one that's always stayed with me."

He tells Kyle and everyone else seated at the table that war story now.

We'd fought a particularly fierce battle this one day, our father began once Neil and I finished with our apologies. Dad crouched at the edge of the marsh, plucked a piece of grass and stuck it between his teeth. As he talked, though he looked out at the marsh, he was seeing another marsh, ten thousand miles away in Southeast Asia. *The gunfire was rampant in that skirmish,* he said. *The VC bold; and the whole bloody mess pretty much a stalemate. Afterward, me and a few comrades eventually rounded a corner out of the jungle to a marsh area along the river. We were exhausted and battle weary, but hell, we were alive and walking. It was early evening and we were following the river back toward camp, making our way through the muck.*

As we walked, we might as well have still been in the jungle. We weren't, but it felt it because of all the green around us. Even the water looked green, winding through the tall marsh grasses. And beyond, the jungle trees rising to the sky were dark green. Every shade of green filled our view. Light, dark, pale, vibrant greens. Sweeping blades of grass, distant trees. Even the inlets through the marsh lapping at the banks as we pressed on. Which made what we saw next even more striking.

Suddenly, the soldier in front of me stopped short. "How do you like that?" he said.

I looked past him. Standing in the mud was a great egret. Statue-still. And brilliant white.

Here we were, dirty and in tatters. Our fatigues soaked through with sweat. Not much left to us at the end of that day. I had my gun up on my shoulder and was making my way through the swampy muck one step at a time. But those steps stopped so I could take in the sight of that tall, white bird. It was so peaceful looking. Pure grace under the fire of a nasty battle of grenades, gunfire, and muzzle flashes that went down all around it the past few hours. Now, none of us moved, not for a good, long time. And I knew why. Seeing that pure white egret, for fleeting minutes we all thought we were back home, at some beach area in the States. Where there was peace. Calm. The simple sight of that white bird brought us there. Brought us home.

We stood there like that, not talking, until a chopper eventually flew past, low to the ground. Those thwacking blades drumming the hot air clearly reminded us of precisely where we actually were: in the middle of a nasty war with no end in sight, and no way out. Every day was just like the one before in that jungle. Sidestepping landmines. Engaging in skirmishes. Hunting the enemy.

But that egret? It stood there in all that green, standing out like a flag of surrender and making no God damn apology for it, either. No apology for being what it was—a white beacon of peace in the midst of that war.

Night Beach

Our father pointed to a white egret standing in the middle of the Stony Point marsh then, near the banks beside the tall grasses. *Never apologize for who you are ... which tonight? I get it. You two were playing soldiers,* he told us. *Which is who you are. Don't apologize for that. No matter what. That bird sure as hell won't. Won't even entertain the notion. But ... You broke curfew, too, which is breaking a rule. So for that, you're grounded. Three days.*

He stood then, and put one hand on my shoulder, one on Neil's. *But never apologize for being yourselves, boys. It has a way of diminishing you.*

―⌒―

Jason looks across the silent table to Kyle. Behind him, floor-to-ceiling windows face the distant Long Island Sound. "It's why I installed an egret stained glass window at Ted Sullivan's place."

"Really," Elsa remarks.

"Sullivan ... Isn't that the fellow who drove the car that hit you and your brother?" Cliff asks. "Had a heart attack at the wheel?"

"Yes, it is. What Ted did that day of the accident was through no fault of his own." Jason raises his glass and sets his gaze directly on Kyle. "And so, I needed no apology from him. And neither do any of us here today, Bradford, from you."

twenty-six

5:45 p.m. – Sunday

THIS IS THE PART OF dinner that Elsa likes best. The platters are nearly empty; dishes a mess of food scraps; chairs pushed back; wineglasses sipped from; candles burning down; talk easy. Like right now, the way Jason, looking tired, sits back with his arm looped over Maris' chair beside him, his fingers toying with his wife's long hair. And the way Paige is scraping the sides of the zucchini casserole bowl for any bits and pieces. Celia sends a text message to Taylor, who is babysitting Aria. Cliff, beside Elsa, takes a long, calm breath. Even Kyle finally relaxed— his dish pushed away as he shows Eva and Matt photos of Chickadee Shanty on his phone.

So with everyone's blood pressure at a nice, comfortable level, Elsa figures now's as good a time as any to spring her thoughts on them. Oh, she knows it, too, that her words will hit like another bomb dropped on this now-placid bunch.

"Cliff, give me a ring-a-ling," she whispers to him.

He squints at her. "What? Why?" he whispers back.

All Elsa does is lightly jab him, so Cliff obliges her request and taps a spoon on his crystal wine goblet.

Yes, it's now or never. When everyone turns to Cliff, Elsa gives a little finger-wave. "Over here," she says with a hopeful smile. "I'm so glad you're enjoying the Sunday dinner today. And now I have something I want to say to you all."

"Aunt Elsa? What is it?" Maris asks.

"Is everything all right?" Eva chimes in as she takes her seat beside Matt.

"Yes. Well," Elsa says. "No. But, please. When you hear what I have to say, just *don't* get mad at me."

Which is when all the moaning and groaning begins—exactly like she knew it would. So she crosses her arms, sits back and lets them all blow their hot air.

Oh, no. No, no, no, Elsa.

Whatever it is, save it.

Not now. Please don't. It'll ruin this incredible dinner.

Stuff it, Elsa.

While they all complain, Elsa simply shakes her head. Outside the floor-to-ceiling windows, the afternoon sun is waning, throwing long shadows on the grounds of her inn. Inside, in the flickering candlelight on the table, the crystal sparkles; the silverware shines; forks scrape last remnants off plates.

And words fly, not stopping until she tips her head down and silently raises her hand.

"I can't put this off, I'm afraid. Today's the day for me to speak. It's why I invited you all here, to my dining room table."

"How do you like that? Even Elsa's got a hidden agenda," Nick fires off.

"Please. Hear me out." Elsa leans forward now, setting her arms on the table. "What it boils down to is this: There's no denying that the weekend was turned on its edge, all by the arrival of one particular man. But I'm having a real hard time reconciling what everyone's told me about Shane Bradford, *and* the reaction to his presence, to what I've actually seen and heard from him."

Silence, then. Pin-drop silence.

Until Jason breaks it. "What?" he asks. "What do you mean ... *heard* from him?"

Elsa looks directly at Jason. "That's right, Jason. I did have a lengthy conversation with Shane last night and—"

"Wait." Jason looks at Cliff now. "Raines? You didn't, you know, dump the coffee and get Shane moving?"

"Now *you* wait. I was completely waylaid by the fine vacationers here yesterday. First there was a raccoon in a garbage pail, and then that beached boat—you saw me there, Jason. Not to mention the speed blocks moved off the road. So, I *did* get Shane out." Cliff pauses before quietly admitting, "But it happened after three in the morning."

"Seriously?" Jason asks. "*That* late?"

With a shrug, Cliff looks at Elsa beside him then and squeezes her hand. "Elsa?" He motions to the table. "Go ahead now."

"Thank you, Cliff," she says before continuing to the now-silent table. And she can see that the friends' silence is evidence of their shock. Shock at how she can think highly of Shane. Still, she loves everyone in this room, and so she tries to explain, clearing her throat before speaking again. "Now, I'm still in the dark about whatever happened years ago with your brother, Kyle. And I'm *not* asking for the story right now. We're all tired after this busy past week and emotions are running high."

After a whispered *Thank God* from someone at the table, and a few sighs of relief, Elsa starts up again. "*But*," she says, "based on what I heard from Shane, I'm just not getting it."

"Getting what?" Vinny asks, his food-laden fork held aloft.

Elsa sips her wine. "I'm just not getting the shunning of the man."

"Neither am I," Nick throws in, and all heads turn to him. "He's all right, seems like a chill dude. I mean, Shane helped me get my Whaler out of the marina last night, on his way to jump-start Cliff's battery."

"What?" Matt asks.

"Cliff?" Jason turns to Cliff again. "You kidding me? Your battery died, too?"

"It did," Cliff answers. "When I had to use my car headlights to safely illuminate the area surrounding the beached sailboat, well, by the time I got back to the car? Those headlights were dark. Drained all the juice from the battery and I—"

Jason brusquely waves off Cliff before he can finish. "Elsa," Jason says, turning to her now. "It's just that we can't have *you* becoming some intermediary here, trying to piece us all back together. Not without knowing the whole story."

"Which nobody could tell me yesterday?" Elsa hears it, the way her voice rises now. Because, yes. Something about this ordeal with Shane *does* get her angry.

"So that *is* what you wanted from me today," Kyle calls across the table, sounding equally angry. "The whole story—"

"I don't think that's what she's saying," Celia manages to squeeze in.

"It's not," Elsa insists. "But Shane was my guest. I had to offer him hospitality, and we talked …" She shifts in her seat and eyes them all. "Okay. Seriously? Here's where I'm struggling. It's mostly with one thing, but it means so much."

"Elsa, you weren't there back when—" Maris tries to explain.

But Elsa won't have it. "No one *ever* told Shane that Neil died?" She doesn't miss it, the way Jason drops back in his chair. The way Kyle expels a breath and looks out the tall window, as though he'd rather be anywhere out there than in here. But she presses everyone gathered at her table. "Because whatever happened between you all, at *one* time Shane was your friend. *And* brother. And if you could've seen him when he learned that news about Neil last night, well … I'd say it was very cruel to somehow not let him know of Neil's passing."

"Listen, Elsa. Please try to understand," Jason says. "So many of us went our separate ways back then."

"It's true. I wasn't even at Neil's funeral, Elsa." Maris turns up her hands. "I was living a different life across the country, building my denim design career."

"Shane, too. He went off lobstering in the Atlantic and wasn't heard from again, for all these years," Matt tells her. "He went and lived his life, with no Stony Point contact."

Kyle leans forward and interrupts. "Elsa. Cliff. What you see here around your table—you know, the friendships, camaraderie—well, this is recent. Wasn't always like this. We have *not* been connected all this time, and really only got back in touch about three years ago."

"Before that, Aunt Elsa," Eva adds, "it was pretty much just me and Matt living here at Stony Point. With Tay. Maris was settled in Chicago, working for Saybrooks. Kyle and Lauren were in Eastfield. Jason had a condo further down the coast. We'd all *lost* touch and hardly talked, believe it or not."

Jason stands to reach over the table for a slice of bread. "A lot happened that summer a few years ago. Maris came back for her father's funeral, and things changed. You know that, Elsa," he reminds her while dragging his bread through tomato sauce on his dish. "That's when Maris found out Eva was actually her sister—after thirty *years* apart."

Elsa's shaking her head. Listening, but shaking her head in some sort of denial. "Yes, yes, I know *that*. But I'm talking about *now*. If you could've seen how withdrawn

Shane got upon learning of Neil's death. It was terribly sad. Someone should've at *least* dropped him a line. Sent an email. Anything ... a few words about the loss of a friend?"

"And then what?" Matt asks.

"Then what?" Elsa shrugs. "Maybe nothing. Maybe it would've just been a common courtesy. Or ... or! Maybe it would've been the start of something. Of fixing things between you all. Because, listen," she loudly says over all their protests. "No, listen. Listen! Shane told me a story about getting on the lobster boats. About how when he's standing on the dock, ready to board and head out to sea. But first, before he gets on the boat? From the docks, he first throws his packed duffel up onto the boat's deck. And that sound, that ... that thud? It's one of the sweetest sounds in the world to him."

"Oh, come on, Elsa," Jason says, waving her story off and nearly knocking down the saltshaker at the same time.

"No, Mr. Barlow. *You* listen. I even pressed him. *Your duffel landing on a boat makes a better sound than birds singing?* I asked him. *Than a loved one's voice?* And do you know what he said?"

"I can imagine," Jason answers, sounding plenty annoyed.

"He told me that being out at sea is a very *authentic* experience. Real, and ... and raw. And that not too many people love the sea, and her wild temperament, the way he does. So much so that the actual thud of his duffel hitting the deck means everything, and here's why: It signifies the beginning of weeks at sea, with no solid ground underfoot.

A place he loves as much as you all love Stony Point, right here."

Celia reaches over and gives Elsa's arm a squeeze. "So what's your point, Elsa?"

"My point is this, Cee. On the day Shane arrived, he brought in that same duffel all loaded and packed. Remember?"

"I do."

"And it was all good, his arrival," Elsa says. "I saw it on his face ... some anticipation, like he must feel when going out lobstering. He seemed happy! He did *not* arrive here—*invited,* I might add—with some evil intent! There was no personal angle. And actually, I must confess, I thought he was happy at the chance to see his brother again. Maybe to see *all* of you again."

"That's bullshit," Kyle quietly says.

"Shane's always been reckless, Elsa," Jason adds. "Getting into trouble, so you can't trust—"

"Well, if Elsa's making confessions," Celia interrupts, standing at her seat now. "I have one to make. And it's that ... I'm *with* Elsa."

"You, too?" Jason asks, tossing up his hands.

"Yes." Slowly, Celia sits again. "After leaving Lauren's last night, I went to the boat basin. Lauren asked me to clear out the wedding flowers in the rowboat there. Shane happened to be on the boardwalk, and must've seen me in the marina. So he helped me remove all the flowers. Said he also wanted to cash in the inn's complimentary rowboat ride voucher. And, well, I owed it to Sal, okay?"

"Sal?" Maris asks.

Celia turns to her. "That's right. Sal was all about second chances. So I gave Shane a *chance* and went out in the rowboat with him last night. And we talked, too. Just like Elsa did," she justifies, pointing at Elsa now. "Which is why I don't get it, either. And Kyle? I actually think you should at least *talk* to your brother."

"Whoa, whoa," Vinny puts in. "Now we're telling people what to do?"

"And I wholeheartedly *disagree* with Celia," Jason says around a mouthful of sauced bread. "One boat ride doesn't show someone's true character. Come on, Celia."

"With my brother on that one," Paige admits.

Matt forks a random stuffed mushroom. "Me, too."

"None of you really get it, though," Kyle calls above the racket. A bead of perspiration lines his face. "What Shane—"

"We get it, just fine," Eva counters. "We were at the bonfire that night—"

"*Bonfire?* What bonfire?" Nick asks. "Where was I?"

"Probably not even born," Matt tosses his way. "It was fifteen years—"

"Fifteen years ago?" Elsa asks. "You mean to tell me you were all in your early twenties when this rift happened?"

"Well, yeah." Eva motions to her sister. "Maris was finishing up college. Taylor was still a toddler. Jason and Neil just started up their architecture and construction business, restoring old cottages." Eva looks down the table with a nod. "And Paige and Vinny were about to get married—"

"But you were in your *twenties*!" Elsa raises an eyebrow. "Need I say more? Because what kind of sound decisions are made at that age? And if you're all this hotheaded now, I can only *imagine* back then!"

"Hotheaded?" Matt asks.

"We have good reason—" Jason tries to argue.

Until a sudden banging silences everyone. The sound raps loudly on the table, and Elsa's surprised to see that it's Cliff, right beside her. He's rising from his seat, and his face is stern as he thumps a serving spoon on her table. "Order … *Order* in the dining room!"

"You know what you can do with that spoon?" Kyle pointedly asks.

Cliff gives another thwack on the table. "*Order*, I said!"

"Not now, Judge," Jason mutters. "Because Shane's a God damn problem, and the truth needs—"

"Wait, guys," Maris cuts in. "A lot of time *has* gone by. Maybe Celia—"

Kyle whips around to Maris. "Celia doesn't know jack—"

When Elsa glares at Kyle, glares at him as she rises from her seat, both hands fisted on the table before her, it's like a curtain drops. Everyone goes silent.

"*Basta!*" Elsa practically hisses. "Enough! *All* of you. This is *my* house, *my* dinner table. And if you can't conduct yourselves in a civilized manner after this most stressful weekend … then please leave. And I *mean* it."

No one moves. At all.

Elsa's glare circles the table until she gets enough reluctant nods to continue. So she sits, sips her wine, and begins again. "That's better. Now, where was I?"

"The duffel …" Cliff prompts.

"Yes, that's right. Shane's duffel story spoke to me, okay? Because when he arrived here at *my* inn, I watched him go upstairs with that very same duffel. I'd just gotten off the phone, and watched as he took those stairs two at a time, with a lightness of step. Shane was actually glad to be here. And when he got upstairs to his bedroom doorway, he must've tossed that duffel into the room the same way he does on the docks—with anticipation of something *good*. Because I heard that duffel *thump* when it hit the floor."

Jason, dragging a crusty piece of his bread through more sauce and cheese on his plate, speaks first. "Okay, fine. You're certainly entitled to your opinion, Elsa." He presses the bread into his mouth. "You've got yours, and we've got ours."

"And nothing's to come of any of it?" Cliff asks.

"That doesn't seem right." Maris reaches over and wipes a crumb from Jason's face.

"Maris." Celia carefully chooses her words. "Lauren invited Shane, and he came willingly. That means something, don't you think?"

"But with Shane gone," Maris counters, "what does it matter now?"

Elsa props her elbows on the table and leans her chin on her clasped hands. "It means, Celia, that we're at an impasse. So it was all for naught, me bringing Shane up like this."

"Maybe, maybe not." Jason hitches his head to Kyle.

"Well, guy? It's your call. Shane's *your* brother. So what do *you* want to do?"

"If I may remind you, Kyle," Elsa interrupts, chin still on hands. "My inn is closed until Labor Day weekend. Which means there's still time, if you can get Shane back here."

Kyle squints over at her. "Here? For what?"

"Instead of your own home, you can use the inn as a neutral territory, a place for you and your brother to talk. To repair your relationship, even." No sooner does she say it than Elsa hears the random groans from the table. For some reason, this crew is just not receptive to a reconciliation.

Kyle takes his napkin and presses it along his forehead. "Listen," he says. "Shane made a choice. He's *left*. Gone. Outta here. And *that* says something, too. If he wanted what you *say* he did, Elsa—peace, or a second chance— he'd have stayed. Maybe would've stuck around a day or two at least. So, I'm thinking we dodged an emotional bullet, actually." Kyle looks over at Nick, and Cliff. "And I don't hold anything against you, for whatever you think of Shane. You know, based on some talks you had. You, too, Celia. *And* Elsa. But my brother's gone now, so a reconciliation wasn't meant to be. For now, please, let's just get on with our own normal lives." He sits back, looking beat with it all. "Let's move on."

"Okay. Decision made," Jason says, wasting no time. "Case closed. We're moving on."

The thing is, when Jason raises his wineglass to toast

Kyle's decision, Elsa notices a hesitation. Not everyone is as quick as you'd expect to join that toast. Oh, they do, but with some resistance, some inner conflict. She sees Nick pause, then shrug and lift his glass with the guys. Cliff doesn't raise his until he sees Elsa oblige with hers. And Maris? Interesting, but Elsa sees how she throws a look from Eva to Jason. Maris hesitates the longest, before barely raising her own glass.

"*Salute*," rings out over the table.

But to Elsa, it's the saddest, most cautious toast she's ever heard declared.

A half hour later, Kyle's feeling even more anxious. He did his best to make amends to all his friends and now he just wants to get back to Lauren at the cabin.

Instead, he's sitting in Elsa's kitchen at her marble-top center island. It doesn't escape him that only a day ago—though it feels like a month—he sat at this very island and whistled a happy tune. Little details come back to him, the moments right before he learned that Shane was in town. Kyle looks around now for the Mason jars wrapped with jute twine, and sees a few empty ones on the counter, beside the toaster. Yesterday he'd sat here, opened one of those twine-wrapped jars and stuffed it with white baby's breath blossoms. The jars were meant to decorate the dinner tables outside the inn, where they'd all eat after his seaside vow renewal ceremony.

Now? Now he's sure those little white blossoms are dead in a trash can somewhere. When Elsa breezes into the kitchen with two large plastic containers in her arms, he doesn't ask about the flowers. "I really have to go, Elsa," he says with a glance at his watch. "Lauren's waiting."

"Okay, I'll hurry." She looks over her shoulder from the counter, where platters of food are laid out. "What would Lauren like, do you think?"

"Lasagna, definitely. And eggplant parmigiana. That's one of her favorites."

"I'll pack some of everything for her. And enough for you, too," Elsa tells him while scooping and lifting large food servings.

"Thanks. That'll be a big help."

"This way, it'll last a few days," Elsa adds. "And you won't have to cook in the cabin. Just heat and eat."

When she snaps on the container lids, Kyle stands up. "Okay. So that's it, then." He leans into the dining room doorway and gives a sweeping wave goodbye to everyone.

But it's not enough. Not for Jason, anyway, who's already standing. Kyle will never forget how Jason tried with all his might to repair, restore or somehow save some scrap of yesterday. So Kyle walks around Elsa's big dining room table, squeezes behind Matt and Eva, and shakes Jason's hand. "Thanks for your help yesterday, guy. It really means a lot."

"Hey, no problem. That's what a best man's for." Jason moves around his chair and gives Kyle a good shoulder slap. "And the hell with us here. You go fix things with your wife now, for crying out loud."

"Do us proud," Vinny calls out, after which someone gives a sharp whistle.

Kyle waves them off and stops in the kitchen again, where Elsa has placed the food containers in a large tote bag. But as he takes them and turns toward the hallway to the front door, Elsa stops him.

"Oh! One more thing, Kyle. Sit, sit." When he grimaces—politely—she motions him toward the kitchen island. "I know you're anxious to get to Lauren. But this'll just take a second," she says, then turns to the counter and carries over another Mason jar—one much bigger than the blossom-filled, vow renewal ones. This one's filled with sand and mini starfish and small scrolls of paper wrapped in ribbon and twine.

"I remember those," Kyle says, nodding to the jar as Elsa sits beside him. "Those are the wishes we made last year?"

"Yes. My wish time capsule. I thought it would be nice if we opened our wishes tonight. Bring some positivity into the weekend."

"But I can't stay."

"I know. So here," she says, reaching into the jar and pulling out the tied scrolls. She reads the names penciled on the outside of each until she finds the right ones. "You take yours. And Lauren's, too. Read them at the cabin and have a little goodness in your evening."

Kyle takes them and unrolls his. "I don't even remember what I wrote." After reading his wish, which seems so sad after this weekend, he also unrolls Lauren's.

"Would you tell me what you wished for?" Elsa whispers.

Kyle looks over at her. Lord knows, Elsa's tried to salvage something from the weekend today. But she looks tired, too. Like they all do. It's obvious she wanted the vow renewal ceremony to happen as much as any of them did. She even had her hair freshly done. Caramel-colored highlights streak her brown hair, which is loosely tied back with a silky scarf. But all she has now, sitting there with her star pendant dangling around her neck, is a shred of hope in her eyes as she waits to hear his wish.

Well, who's Kyle to deny anyone their hope? Especially after he squelched everyone's this weekend. So he hands Elsa Lauren's wish, first.

"It's Ell's," he says. "Very touching."

Elsa looks around, then spots her leopard-print reading glasses over on the counter. "Do you remember what Lauren did when she rolled up her wish last year?" she asks while putting on those glasses.

Kyle looks at her and shakes his head.

"She lifted it to her face and kissed it ... with such tenderness," Elsa quietly says. Then she unrolls the paper and murmurs Lauren's words. *"Twinkle lights on, every night, on the porch. That kind of life ..."*

She gives Kyle a sad smile when he hands her his wish next. As she opens it, Kyle hears the voices in the dining room. They're starting to relax again. Jason's talking about his Castaway Cottage episodes, and what's next in the filming. Eva actually sold a house this morning. Vinny's telling someone the classes he'll be teaching in September at the high school.

But Kyle, beside Elsa, remains silent.

Lowering her glasses on her nose, Elsa whispers his wish now. "*Happy family memories at our new beach home.*"

The two wishes, his and Lauren's, are enough to choke her up. Kyle can see that when she glances away, pulls off her glasses and presses the back of her hand to her eyes. Well, who wouldn't want all that, *a twinkle-lights kind of life?* Oh, isn't it something so small, and so huge, all at once. Hell, if Kyle dwells on it, he'll just about choke up, too.

Thankfully, Elsa doesn't allow him a moment to. Instead she rolls up both wishes, slips the twine back on each, and gives the papers to Kyle. Then she wraps her arms around him in a big hug, surprising in its intensity.

"Go!" she says, motioning him to the inn's front door while swiping away another tear. "Go now! And be with Lauren."

twenty-seven

7:00 p.m. – Sunday

It FEELS FUNNY SLICING THE wedding cake. After putting on her glasses, Elsa presses a knife through another piece. Wedding cake cutting should be merry. There should be *Whoops!* And smiles. And tender touches. The newlyweds should gently feed a taste of sweet cake to each other, then dab any crumbs off their faces, maybe brush away a happy tear, too.

Instead, the kitchen is quiet as Elsa slices yesterday's untouched cake. A lone robin chirrups outside her garden window. On the sill, her tiny red pails overflow with fresh herbs: rosemary, basil and such. Everyone's still here, but she'd shooed them out onto the deck off the old Foley's back room. That's where the coffeepot is set up, and the cups, and cream and sugar. Not to mention, what better place to open all their year-old wishes than beneath the stars?

"Aunt Elsa? Can I help you with that?"

Standing at her massive kitchen island, Elsa lowers her reading glasses and glances over her shoulder. "Oh, Maris." Her niece is dressed casually, wearing a wide leather belt with her favorite cuffed jeans, a fitted tee half tucked, her star necklace hanging from a braided gold chain around her neck. Her hair, curled into waves yesterday for the big event, is straight tonight. "I'm all set here. You just keep me company," Elsa tells her, nodding to a stool at the island.

"It's sad, isn't it?" Maris asks while sitting and reaching for a cake slice. "This weekend."

"It is." Elsa keeps slicing the wedding cake. "But these things happen sometimes. Not often, but sometimes."

In a quiet pause, a warm sea breeze comes in through the kitchen window. There are voices, too, carrying to Elsa from the deck. Laughs now, and conversation, as the evening winds down.

"You mentioned talking to Shane earlier," Maris says then.

"We had a long chat outside last night. With coffee."

Maris picks at the cake slice. "How'd he seem?" she asks, mid-nibble.

"A little guarded." Elsa stops slicing to brush a strand of hair from her face. "But pleasant. Even though he was really taken aback by the fallout of the day. Because how could he expect this would happen? Especially when he *was* invited—which he thought was all cleared by Lauren *and* Kyle."

"I know. Anyone would've thought that."

"That's right."

"Elsa?"

Elsa glances at Maris, who's dabbing a finger into the icing on her cake slice.

"Did Shane talk about his summers at Stony Point?" Maris asks.

"He did, a little bit." Elsa cuts two more white-frosted slices. "Mentioned some memories with Kyle. Something about stone-skipping competitions they used to have."

"That's it? Nothing about his old friends here?"

"Not really. Not at first. Mostly he talked about his job as a lobsterman." Elsa steps to the side and sets another few slices of cake onto a serving platter, then uses a napkin to wipe off her cutting knife. "Seafaring tales," she says as she resumes cake-cutting, "from out on the water. He reminded me so much of Sal."

"Sal?"

"Mm-hmm. The way Shane lives his work *so* fully? Sal was like that, too. So I actually enjoyed talking with Shane." When Maris says nothing, Elsa looks up at her. From her niece's expression, her thoughts seem to be elsewhere. "He was rather drawn to that photograph in the back room. The one of all of you, from last summer? When Sal was still here."

"Oh, I'm sure he was. Shane hasn't seen the gang together for fifteen years now. And he was once such a part of it. It must've felt odd seeing us like that, all these years later."

"A couple of things in that picture really surprised him." After setting a few more cake slices on the platter, Elsa looks long at Maris. "You, especially."

"Me?"

"Yes. That you gave up denim design to settle here in this, as *he* called it, harbor town."

"Well." Maris shifts on her stool and tucks her hair behind an ear. "He'd have no way of knowing where my life took me."

"I guess not, being out at sea the way he is. *And* with whatever rift came between you all. But still. I *was* truly shocked that he didn't at least know about Jason and Neil. That nobody told him. It still seems cold to me, excluding an old friend from such tragic news."

Maris gives a slight shrug. "You have to understand. We really did go our separate ways, like we said earlier. Even I was living halfway across the country when Jason and Neil were in the accident. I missed the funeral, Kyle and Lauren's wedding, *and* Jason's recovery. Eva filled me in on things back then, but I only learned the details when I came back three years ago … long after it happened." She shoves the rest of her cake into her mouth, then pats her lips with a napkin. "I was wondering, though. Did Shane say where he was going when he left here?" she asks around her chewing.

"No." Again, from where she stands at the island, Elsa eyes Maris sitting across from her. "And is there a reason *you're* asking so many questions?"

Maris looks right back at her. Looks away next, down

the hall in the direction of the deck where everyone else is. Finally, she jumps off her stool and turns to Elsa again. "Okay. I'm going to tell you something, Aunt Elsa. But … you must look me in the eye and promise it's our secret." She takes a step closer. "Promise?"

Seeing Maris' dark eyes so serious with a forbidden story of her own, Elsa nods. "Of course, Maris! I promise. But something seems wrong …"

"It's not. Not now, anyway." Maris hurries around the grand marble-top island to where Elsa still stands. Stopping right beside her, as close as she can get, Maris drops her voice. "And if *anyone* walks in, we change the subject. Real quick."

"Maris." Elsa sets down her cake knife, raises her leopard-print glasses to the top of her head and turns to her niece. "This sounds serious. Is everything okay?"

"Yes. But there *is* something you should know." Again, Maris squints at Elsa, then leans close, cups her hands and whispers into Elsa's ear. "*Shane and I … we were going to be married.*"

"*What?*" Elsa harshly whispers back.

Maris quickly nods, a finger to her lips. "*It was a long time ago, and nobody really knew,*" she still whispers. "*But we were briefly engaged, until I kind of broke things off. And maybe broke his heart.*" A sad smile comes before Maris adds, "*My own heart, too.*"

Elsa quickly drags a stool over and sits on it. "Maris! So *you're* the one. Shane mentioned that he'd been—"

"Ladies?"

Both women whip around to see Jason turning into the kitchen and snagging a piece of sliced cake. "What's going on?" he asks around a mouthful of the frosted pastry.

"Oh." Maris looks at Elsa, then at her husband. "Jason—"

"We were just deciding who would water Lauren's, um … window boxes," Elsa lies. Slickly. Without batting an eye. Which Maris must notice. Because she reaches over and discreetly taps Elsa's gold bangle. Just like that, they are in cahoots.

"Right, her new window boxes," Maris adds while watching Jason polish off his cake in two big bites.

"We'd hate to see her geraniums wilt while she and Kyle are away." With that, Elsa tosses an easy smile Jason's way and cuts one last slice of cake.

"Got it. Well, do you need a hand here?" Jason asks, motioning to Elsa's now-overloaded dessert platter.

"Yes, that would be wonderful. It's about time for dessert, so can you carry that cake tray out to the deck?" Elsa asks, then subtly motions for Maris to wait.

Jason, who Elsa thinks may or may not have seen her signal, lifts the tray of white-frosted cake slices.

"Come on, sweetheart," he says over his shoulder to Maris.

Maris looks at Elsa, shrugs and mouths, *Later*.

twenty-eight

7:50 p.m. — Sunday

JASON BARLOW LEANS AGAINST THE deck railing. It's one of his favorite spots at Stony Point, mostly because it's where he fell in love with Maris one August night fifteen years ago. The old Foley's joint was closing up for good back then, so the gang had one last get-together in their hangout. On the deck, Jason ended up slow-dancing with Maris to a jukebox song, and kissed her once before the night was through.

So keeping that deck intact was important to Jason—and worth every minute of quibbling with his aunt-through-marriage. He spent the entire summer last year fine-tuning inn design plans with Elsa. They haggled most over the turret *and* this expansive deck off the original Foley's back room.

As he leans against the deck railing now, Jason remembers how they nitpicked. How far should the deck extend from beneath the roof overhang? *A nice amount*, Elsa suggested, pointing to his blueprint. *No*, Jason countered. *A significant amount, for a significant beach inn.* They split hairs over the deck posts. *Natural cedar, and matching the shingles?* Jason asked. *No, white*, Elsa insisted. *Brilliant in the sunshine.* Back and forth they went. *But... No, because... How about... I'm telling you, this is better... What do you think of... I prefer this.*

The real sticking point that tested their working relationship, though, came with the deck's door selection. From inside the inn, the deck would be accessed only through a door off that back room.

The door must be substantial, Elsa demanded. *With wide white trim matching the window trim. I'd like French doors, actually. Double doors, paned.* On this issue, her tone was serious, and unyielding.

And Jason's headshake was just as obstinate. *May I remind you of the contract stipulation you signed off on? The one stating the back room's design remains unchanged?* Which was followed by more *Buts* and *Not in this instance* and *It won't work that way.*

Until Jason won. That binding contract stipulation was included for exactly this reason—to ensure that the back room's original architecture, and so its memories, would live on. *The only door I'll consider is the original squeaking, wood-framed screen door*, Jason flat-out told her. *My crew will get it all gussied up for you. New screens, hinges. The works.*

To which Elsa threw up her hands in defeat.

Tonight, with Maris beside him on the new deck a year later, Jason looks out toward the distant view of the beach. The sky is pale red at the horizon; Long Island Sound, gray.

Night Beach

It's instinct, really, the way it happens. The way he fills his lungs with a deep breath of that salt air while looking at the sea. When he does, Maris loops her arm through his and leans close. Don't they think alike, knowing this view, this air, shapes most of their days.

When they turn a moment later, Jason sees how the deck is illuminated with candles and hanging paper lanterns.

"Magical, isn't it?" Maris' voice is soft. "Especially at sunset."

Guests are spearing hunks of white-frosted wedding cake. The talk is low-key, laughs frequent enough, beneath the twilight sky. "To any passing stranger," Jason says to Maris, "this would look like a bona fide wedding reception. Dessert outside, twinkly lights, music, good cheer."

But Jason knows better. He hears what a stranger wouldn't. He hears the quiet pauses in the talk. Hears the worried words about Kyle and Lauren. Sees the watch-checking. Hears hushed mention of Shane. So all is not at ease. Not yet.

Not until tomorrow, he figures, when everyone will return to their normal workaday lives. To familiar routine.

Which makes the weekend feel all the more futile. There's something regretful about it, all of it—even the wedding-cake dessert. Because instead of being served in celebration, the cake's doled out simply so that too much food doesn't go to waste.

And, well? Cake or not, Jason's sure everyone here would be happier to just forget that the whole disastrous weekend even happened.

Inside the back room, Elsa stands in shadow. It gives her a chance to watch all her loved ones out on the deck. Which surprisingly breaks her heart. The jukebox plays a slow tune behind her, the music carrying outside through the open windows. But music or not, no one's dancing. Jason and Maris stand off by themselves. Vinny quietly works on a big slice of cake. Taylor brought Aria from the guest cottage, and now Celia sets the baby's bouncy seat on a table, then sips her coffee while chatting with Matt and Eva. Even Cliff and Nick seem withdrawn. Standing side by side with arms crossed, they lean on the deck railing and force some small talk.

So maybe Elsa's Sunday dinner only prolonged the sadness of yesterday. Eating leftover reception food, serving some of the vow renewal cake rather than throw it away—it's just a painful reminder of all that fell apart. Not to mention, Maris' secret about Shane, and their past engagement, has Elsa worried now, too.

When a sea breeze carries through the screen door, Elsa tips her head. *Sorridi*, she thinks she hears whispered. *Smile, Ma.* Oh, wouldn't Sal turn on his own smile and somehow salvage the weekend.

But now, that responsibility falls to her. So she opens the wood-framed screen door and dashes outside, the squeaking door slamming shut. The *least* she can do is try to change the mood.

And try she does. Elsa crosses the deck with a large happiness jar in one hand; a basket holding tiny seashells, uncooked spaghetti and a lighter in the other. She's determined to do her best to weave some thread of hope into this still-sad night.

"Remember this?" Elsa calls out. She waves everyone closer to the deck tables. Patio umbrellas are opened over each. White lights strung around the umbrella spokes cast a glow on the tables. As chairs are pulled out and the guests all take a seat, Elsa holds up the Mason jar filled with small scrolls of paper tucked into fine beach sand. "This is our wish capsule," she says. "You all wrote down your hopes and dreams last October, when I had you to dinner. We were celebrating my decision to *not* sell this beach inn."

"I remember," Vinny says, raising a fork toppling with cake. "And a great night it was."

"Absolutely," Cliff adds, approaching Elsa's table. "Can I help you with something there, Elsa?"

"Yes." She hands Cliff the lighter before talking to all her guests again. "When I'd committed to my inn that night last year, I also explained its name: Ocean Star Inn. A name picked special for my sister, June, who believed that twinkling *ocean* stars—when sunlight sparkles on the sea—are as magical as night stars. And who doesn't love wishing on a star, *any* star? So I'd asked you all to make a secret wish that night, in honor of June. And of the stars above, and on the sea. Back then, we tied up our wishes and promised not to open them for one year. But tonight? Tonight I think we all need a reason to believe in happiness. In hopes and dreams."

Matt gives a sharp whistle cutting through the evening air, and a few people agree with an *Absolutely!* and *Do we ever!*

"Okay," Elsa says, nodding to them. "So that's why I thought we should actually untie and reveal our wishes together. Beneath the summer sky."

"Tonight?" Eva asks. "I understand what you're saying—"

"But it hasn't been a full year," Maris finishes. "Are you *sure* you don't want to wait, Aunt Elsa?"

"Yes, I'm sure." Elsa looks out toward the distant seascape, its horizon darkening now. "We all need to smile … *tonight*." With that, she picks up the Mason jar that has sat beside a basket of seashells on her painted hutch in the dining room. "This was the first official happiness jar of the Ocean Star Inn," Elsa says while opening the lid. She tips the jar to the side and pulls out all the scrolled-and-tied wishes, leaving only beach sand and a few mini starfish inside. "So let's put that happiness to work."

"I'll freshen our coffees," Eva says, standing and getting the coffeepot, "while you distribute the wishes."

"Oh, I'll do that!" Maris jumps up and takes the paper wishes.

"The names are written on the outside of each," Elsa tells her. "And while you hand out the wishes, I'll put a candle in the empty happiness jar." She sets a silver candle in the sand, then lifts a spaghetti strand. "One small flame," she explains, "will help us find some light this dark weekend." With that, she motions for Cliff to hold the lighter to the tip of her uncooked spaghetti strand. When the flame takes, Elsa dips the burning spaghetti piece in the jar and carefully lights the candle's wick. After snuffing the spaghetti tip, she does one more thing: sprinkles a handful of tiny white seashells around the flickering candle before setting the magical jar on the deck railing. There, it glimmers against the darkening blue sky behind it.

"Okay?" Elsa turns and asks Maris. "All distributed?"

"Yes. Let the wishes unfold," Maris tells her while sitting close beside Jason again.

"And please. I'd like to go first," Elsa states as Eva works her way around the patio tables and finally fills Elsa's coffee cup. Once Elsa sits beside Cliff, she lowers the leopard-print reading glasses from the top of her head and unties her wish. "With so many tumultuous days after Sal's death last summer," she begins while unrolling her scrolled paper, "this was my small, personal wish." She leans to Cliff so he can see it, too, before reciting her wish aloud. "Smooth sailing in the year ahead, for all." When Elsa looks up at everyone watching her with some shred of hope, with small smiles on their faces, her eyes well up. "Easy peace ... for everyone."

⁓

If at all possible, what Jason notices is that the deck gets even quieter once Elsa reads her wish. Twine-tied scrolls are dropped, or fidgeted with. Celia, sitting with Eva and Matt, wipes a tear from her face. Cliff clasps Elsa's arm and whispers in her ear.

"Maybe we shouldn't read these today," Jason says.

"I think so, too. It doesn't feel right," Paige agrees, then sips from her coffee. Sitting with Vinny, she pulls a light cardigan up over her shoulders. "So I'm with Jason, Elsa."

"Me, too," Celia pipes in. "Because if our wishes *didn't* come true this past year, it'll only make us sadder."

"But my wish *did* come true," Elsa explains while pulling off her glasses and setting them aside.

Which is when Jason sees it. Sees some resolve. Because, oh no. No, no, no. The adamant Elsa DeLuca he knows—as usual—is not one to back down.

"Smooth sailing and easy peace?" Elsa asks. She walks to Celia's table, where Aria wears a polka-dot romper and a small bow in her dark hair. The baby kicks her chubby legs and bats at felt animals strung across her bouncy seat. "Peace is all I *have* when I set my eyes on my precious new granddaughter, Aria." Elsa lightly touches the baby's cooing face before squeezing Celia's shoulder.

But Elsa's not done—not that Jason thought she would be. Quickly, she turns to another table. His. "And, and *Jason*! Jason, you have your TV show!"

Jason turns up his hands in reluctant agreement. He also watches Elsa-in-action, trying to convince them of their happiness. When she motions to Maris next, Elsa's gold bangle spins on her wrist; her star necklace shimmers in the V of her long black blouse; her sandaled feet skim the deck floor with insistent steps.

"Maris is finishing Neil's *novel*," Elsa goes on when she returns to her seat beside Cliff. "And Kyle and Lauren? Well, they're finally settled in their beautiful beach home. So my wish for smooth sailing for *all* … Isn't it obvious?

In recent months, we were all *there*, on some buoyant sea. Good things were coming our way. So … so the waters got choppy for a few days this week, but it was just … a blip."

"A dirty day," Celia quietly adds.

"A what?" several voices ask.

Jason turns to the table where Celia's sitting. "A *dirty* day?" he repeats.

Celia nods. "Shane actually told me about them, yesterday. That's how he described nasty days at sea."

"Interesting way to put it," Maris remarks.

"I thought so. You know, those days with terrible conditions that a lobsterman has to fight through. Wind, and high seas. Waves washing right over the boat, the salt water drenching you through as you struggle to even stand straight. Dirty days, he called them. And that's what it feels like *we* had, yesterday. A dirty day. One that wanted to knock us right down." Celia gives a hopeful smile. "But we'll get through ours, too?" She looks around at all of them. "Lauren and Kyle are already trying."

"Okay. I like that … getting through a dirty day," Cliff announces. "We've certainly done it before, and can do it again. So I'll go next."

As soon as Cliff's untying his scrolled wish, Jason notices a change. And all because of a random sea story Shane told Celia. Now Nick's leaning way back in his chair to bullshit some nonsense with Vinny. Eva's laughing at whatever Matt's telling her. Maris' hand rubs Jason's arm.

Suddenly they're all yakking and letting loose a bit.

So something about surviving a *dirty day* has them feeling optimistic.

Something about Shane brings that out.

But they all quiet when Cliff loudly clears his throat. He holds his wish in front of him, then moves it farther out and squints while reading. "Advance my wooing of a certain Mrs. DeLuca." He drops his hand when a few hoots and hollers come his way. "Which is my wish-in-progress," he adds, then throws Elsa a wink.

You've got to step it up, Commish, someone calls out.

Put a ring on it, for crying out loud! another voice persists.

Jason sits back and takes it all in. With the twilight sky getting darker so that tiny stars emerge, the air seems more charged. A breeze lifts off the Sound, touching his face. The wish candle glimmers in the Mason jar set on the deck railing.

But it's Nick who gets his attention next when he scrapes his chair back and stands. "If I can have your attention over here," Nick begins. "And a drumroll, please," he adds while unrolling his scrolled wish. Vinny obliges, rapping his hands rapidly on the table. "That was legit, Vincenzo. And now? The moment of truth. My big wish reveal … Hoping to have my own personal digs," Nick reads. In the silence that follows, he looks at everyone, gives a slight bow and sits again.

"That's it? You mean you want your own place?" Matt asks. "Like … an apartment?"

"I could find you a cottage, right here! Happen to know a great realtor," Eva says while pointing to herself.

"You might want to consider using Eva's services, Nicholas. Because a *boat* doesn't quite qualify as living quarters," Cliff reminds him, making mention of Nick's used Boston Whaler.

Nick squints over at him. "That boat's my *own* space anyway, boss. Even if it *is* on the water."

Oh, Jason sees it, how Cliff brushes him off. The commish is obviously aware that Nick might very well be onto Cliff's *secret* digs in the Stony Point Beach Association trailer.

And so it goes. The ribbing starts up. The friendly jabs, too. Then there are the smiles upon reading the wishes. The nodding when hearing the words. The briefly closed eyes of, yes, of some small hope.

So Elsa was right. The wishes work: from Matt wishing to save enough money by next summer to "find me a sweet RV for Tay's college tours," to Eva saying she only wished to spruce up her realty—now known as *By the Sea Realty*—to Maris wishing not only to complete Neil's half-written manuscript, but to do right by it.

"Still time, sis." Eva rushes over to give Maris a hug. "We opened these wishes early, so there's two months left to go," Eva reminds her.

Which gets everyone asking Maris about the book, and if they're in it, and how does it feel mixing her own words with Neil's.

It's Celia's wish, though, that brings quiet again. Wearing an ankle-length sundress, there's something about the way she stands at her table that does it. A few auburn wisps from her topknot brush her face as she pauses, stock-still. Celia waits, simply watching them until someone shushes the crowd. Finally, she unrolls her wish.

"To smile more," Celia reads, looking at each of them. "For Sal."

Sorridi, several voices call out, prompting Elsa to pat her heart upon hearing her son's catchphrase.

"And I *have* smiled." Celia reaches to the bouncy seat on the table and touches Aria's little hand. "I definitely have," she whispers, then bends and kisses her daughter's cheek.

In a moment, Cliff taps a spoon to his mug. "Only one wish left," he announces. "Jason?"

"Oh, *Jason*." Elsa hurries to his table and sits across from him. "You were the very last one to write your wish last year. I remember. And I wondered most about what *your* wish might be."

"About mine?" Jason asks, lifting his tied-up wish.

Elsa nods.

"Why mine?"

"Last summer was so special, with Sal here for all those months. Smiles were plentiful; life was good." Elsa motions out past the deck railing to the twilight-blue sky, then turns to Jason again. "After I worked closely with you on the inn's redesign during that time, well, you felt like a son to me, too. So especially after we all reeled from Sal's loss, I wanted to know where you saw *your* life going."

Jason looks over his shoulder when Nick stands and moves closer, leaning against the nearby deck railing while sipping his coffee and watching him. Matt and Eva turn in their chairs, too, Jason notices. Paige and Vinny raise their coffee cups in a toast to him.

And Maris? She brushes the side of his face and drags her fingers through his hair.

So Jason does it. All the while, he hears the whispering around him. Hears voices nudging him to hurry up. Slowly, he unrolls the paper, silently reads his wish, then sets his hand down and nods with a small smile at the only wish that mattered to him last year.

Still is the only wish that matters. Always will be.

"Come on, guy," Matt calls out.

Jason glances at them before opening the paper again. "More jukebox dances with my wife," he reads, then reaches for Maris' hand and kisses the back of it—holding it to his lips for a long second.

The tables quiet once his wish is read. There's only that slight sea breeze, and faint starlight in the dusky evening sky. And on the deck railing? The silver candle set in golden sand flickers in the clear glass jar.

twenty-nine

10:00 p.m. – Sunday

KYLE WATCHES LAUREN. SHE DOESN'T say anything, but when you really know someone, every nuance about them carries a message. He catches those nuances in certain glimpses of his wife as they sit outside near the firepit with a glass of wine. It's in the way Lauren's hand slightly moves her glass to get the wine swirling. When they later close up Chickadee Shanty for the night, Kyle sees more of her unspoken nuances. As Lauren rinses a few dishes and glasses in the kitchen sink. As she extinguishes the lantern on the fireplace mantel, then bends for the aroma of the lavender stems in the pail there. The way she checks that the cabin's front door is locked. Her every nuance tells him something.

Yes, while Kyle shuts off the birch-bark chandelier and table lamps near the plaid sofa, he finally knows. By the lightness of her hands, and her step, he can tell Lauren doesn't regret being here.

But what's in her reluctant smile is some sad disappointment that they just couldn't get here under better circumstances.

So he tries his best to maybe make her scrolled wish come true. *Twinkle lights on every night.* Fortunately, some of those tiny white lights are strung in the cabin. Not many, but enough. Entwined through the branchlets hung over the fireplace. And tacked over the front door.

To grant her wish, Kyle leaves only those lights glimmering in the darkness.

Even when Lauren takes off her wire bracelets—silently, but gently—in the cabin bedroom, there's no tension in her fingers as she sets them on the small wooden dresser. And her hair? She pulls the brush through it, easily, after putting on her satin nightshirt.

It isn't until she climbs into bed, though, that he does it. That Kyle sits beside her and gives her the two scrolled wishes.

"What's this?" Lauren asks.

Kyle gets under the sheet and lies next to her. He strokes her hair, looks at her eyes. "Our wishes, from last year."

"The ones we wrote at Elsa's? When she decided to keep the inn?"

Kyle only nods. "Go ahead," he whispers, hitching his head to her twined wish.

"Tonight? But Elsa said we shouldn't open them for a year."

"She changed her mind. Everyone was going to open theirs tonight. I left before that, but Elsa thought we could all use a little happiness. So she gave me these, to open here."

Lauren looks long at Kyle before handing him one scrolled wish. "You go first."

"Okay." Kyle turns and plumps his pillow before lying on his back. This seems a nice place to share their wishes, in this secluded lakeside cabin. They have no other memories here to taint their hopes; no bombshell news flashes in their lives; no arguments here; no friends coming around; no cell phones on this unplugged stay.

No lapping waves, either. No cry of the gulls. No hitching, salty breeze.

Their getaway at this shanty in the woods is as pure, as untarnished by their own complicated lives, as can be.

So he unties the twine and unrolls his wish. Beside him, Lauren settles beneath the sheet and watches. He looks at her, then at his hopeful words. Can they get there? Can he and Lauren pull things together and begin making memories again? Good memories. He takes a deep breath and reads his wish. "Happy family memories at our new beach home," he says, his voice cracking.

Then? Nothing. Still holding the wish, he lowers his hand and closes his eyes. Long moments pass when Lauren doesn't even move. But he feels the bed shift when she eventually unrolls her wish. And even though he's afraid to see her expression when she reads the words hoped for a year ago—words he just about wiped off the map with his temper yesterday—he turns his head and watches her.

She doesn't look at him, though. She just reads her

words. "Twinkle lights on, every night, on the porch. That kind of life." As if remembering the moment she wrote those words, she gives a slight nod.

After that, the bedroom is quiet; the patchwork quilt folded to the foot of the bed. That owl *hoot-hoots* far out in the woods, its call muted. The air presses close within the wood-planked walls. Kyle's breathing feels labored. But when he glances around, he notices something. The beams crisscrossing the bedroom ceiling have tiny lights on them, too. So he reaches over, takes Lauren's scrolled paper from her hand and sets both their wishes, twine and all, on the bedside table. Without a look back, he gets out of bed, switches off the nightstand lamp and flips a switch on the wall, near the door.

It does what he'd hoped. The little white lights twinkle above. After looking up at them for a long second, he gets back into bed, saying nothing.

Neither does Lauren.

But it doesn't matter, because he can read her nuances.

And he can feel them when she reaches over and turns his head toward her, leans close and kisses him. Her hands cradle his face as she kisses his mouth, his jaw, his tear-filled eyes, then his mouth again, deeper this time. She presses her body closer, slips a leg over him and sits up, straddling him. When she takes his hand in hers—her nuances clear—she lowers his hand to the hem of her satin nightshirt and helps him lift it, slowly, over her head. Her blonde hair falls loosely over her shoulders as the fabric is pulled off; silver chains glimmer on her neck; her breasts are soft as his hands skim over them; as she bends to kiss him again.

Well. One thing Kyle Bradford knew damn well was that his month-long vow of celibacy wouldn't end at *his* doing. Not after what he put his sweet Ell through these past couple of days.

But that vow is about to end, right now. At Lauren's invitation; at her seduction beneath the lights twinkling on the ceiling beams.

When she helps him slip off his pajama bottoms before mounting him again, he knows something else, too. When she leans low—her hands on his shoulders, her kiss on his mouth—yes, he knows it then.

He knows now that somehow, they'll get there.

Their wishes stand a chance.

Because it's the very last thing he sees before her silky hair falls forward. The last thing he sees before her hands move down his chest, his sides—her soft kisses following her touch. There on the nightstand, he caught a fleeting glimpse. Scarcely illuminated by those tiny ceiling lights, are their two paper wishes, curled at the edges, twine tangled over them.

As he feels every bit of Lauren on top of him, as his hands move up the smooth skin of her bare back before tangling in her hair, he whispers between kisses how much he loves her. And he could sob with relief when, lowering herself on him fully, Lauren whispers back that she loves him, too.

Only the nightlight is on in Aria's room. For the third time in the past hour, Celia tiptoes in, stands by the crib and looks down at her baby daughter. Aria's little hands are loosely fisted in sleep; her eyelashes brush her face.

The first two times Celia checked on her baby, she lightly swept her fingers over Aria's fine hair, toying with a curl of it for a moment.

This time, Celia instead walks to the window, lifts her hand and jingles the seashell wind chime hanging there. Usually she thinks of Sal when she does that, and the night he hung this wind chime in the little marsh-side cottage she'd been staying at. *Serenata le stelle*, he'd said in Italian as the seashell strings clinked and clattered. *Serenading the stars*, he whispered then, waltzing her across the floor.

Tonight she doesn't think of Sal.

No. She thinks of Shane instead, rowing her across the sea, beneath the stars. Little details stay with her, like his hands holding the oars, his tattoos visible as his arms worked those oars through the water. His hands are so obviously working hands: strong ... and firm. Sure of their grip. Yet so gentle when he helped remove Lauren's sad wedding flowers from the rowboat.

Was it only two days ago that Celia met Shane Bradford? Two days since she stopped at the reservation desk when Elsa checked him into the inn? Celia held Aria in her arms, and she remembers one of Shane's strong hands delicately tapping Aria's hand that morning.

The lobsterman and the baby. His love of the sea. His nostalgia for this little beach. Hints of a long-vanquished chip on his shoulder. Dirty days. The sound of a duffel-toss holding certain meaning, to only him.

How can she know so much about him in so little time?

She gives the seashells another nudge, clinking the shells together, then looks out at the night. Over the beach, the moon rises, its silver illumination falling on the water beneath it. She stands there, looking out and hoping Shane's okay.

And feeling just a bit sad that after their own moonlit row, after their quiet talk beneath the starry night sky, she didn't get to tell him goodbye.

Jason and Maris were last to leave Elsa's. They helped her clean up the deck patio tables, got the dishwasher loaded and wiped down the kitchen.

"Thanks, Aunt Elsa," Maris told her when she hugged Elsa goodbye. "I think it helped, all of it. The dinner with everyone, *and* those special wishes."

"It always helps to be together. To lean on each other," Elsa reminded them as they took a bag of leftovers and waved goodbye.

It's late when Jason finally pulls into their driveway, the SUV's tires snapping over a few fallen twigs. He parks and walks across the dark yard with Maris, onto the deck, and inside to the kitchen. The dog is right there at them, tail wagging, nails clicking on the floor, winding her way between them until Jason says he'll feed her.

"Okay, babe. I'll put the leftovers in the fridge," Maris tells him when she drops her purse on the counter.

After getting the dog settled, Jason walks down the paneled hallway, past the dining room where the lantern-chandelier casts a soft light. On the table beneath it, two pillar candles sit on wide, silver pedestals.

The same, same as always. Everything the same.

Yet *something's* different tonight. Like they're all feeling vulnerable after witnessing how swiftly circumstances can change; love can change.

Lives, too, Jason thinks when he turns into the living room and sits on the upholstered chair beside the stone fireplace. Propped on the mantel, beside a few tin stars, is the framed photograph of him and Neil leaning on the railing of the old Foley's deck. His brother loosely holds a beer. His wavy hair lifts in a sea breeze. Yes, lives change, too. Too swiftly.

In a while, Maris brings in glasses of wine, sets them on an end table and turns to the side alcove and the vintage jukebox there. Its silver trim glimmers in the low light, and she pauses in front of it. Jason watches her while sipping his wine. Wearing her favorite cuffed jeans and leather sandals, a fitted tee and her star necklace, she runs a finger over the glass while making a selection.

In the dim lighting, it's beautiful, all of it. His wife, the needle hitting the record. When Maris turns to him with open arms, Jason pauses, then stands and goes to her. Yes, a beautiful moment … but different, somehow, this dance they begin now. When he takes Maris in his arms, she whispers his name. The jukebox needle settles on the old record, and a melancholy song about missing sweet loving begins.

Their dance does, too. Slowly, their bodies pressing close, they move around the room. As Jason holds his wife, as his fingers tangle in her brown hair, he sees how she lit the dining room candles earlier; they flicker in the darkness.

And he gets it, why he made that wish last year. Dancing to scratchy jukebox tunes with his wife like this? It's enough. It's his happiness. Not too long ago, it was more than he thought he'd ever have—holding his Maris in this big old beach house full of memories and spirits and plenty of love now. He hears Maris' hushed sweet nothings murmured near his ear. The two of them sway as slightly as the sea breeze making its way through the open windows.

But tonight the moment isn't really about the dance. Jason feels it. It's more like that night blindness his father talked about. None of them are really sure of what's to come anymore, not after the turn this weekend took for Kyle and Lauren. Now they all can't see beyond what's right in front of them.

So tonight's about holding on to whoever's there.

Jason does it himself when Maris raises her head from his shoulder. He touches her face, drags his fingers down her neck and kisses her for a long moment. It's a kiss when Maris loops her fingers through his belt loops and leans in close. When her own kiss grows serious. Needy, even.

Later, in their bedroom, Jason still feels it, that clinging. That holding on. Maris starts taking off his shirt from behind when he's still sitting in his bedside chair, bent over and not even done removing his prosthetic leg. Once he moves to the bed, he gets her cuffed jeans and tee off just as quickly—their clothes tossed aside, his hands pressing her down on the mattress, the bed covering not folded back. When they make love, they're greedy. In the darkness, touches insist. Maris' kisses move, and surprise. On top of her, Jason's arms restrain her. Breathing is rapid. Words are few. The sex is urgent. Afterward, sleep comes right away with Maris pressed close beside him, her hand on his chest, his arm around her shoulders.

Elsa stands at the deck railing and looks out over the distant night beach. There's a haze around the nearly full moon. It looks as evocative as the night sometimes felt with everyone gathered here on the old Foley's deck. The sight of those twined wishes being unrolled beneath the dark August sky was mystical. And after a tense dinner when the arguing about Shane tainted much of the evening, those happy wish-moments on the deck didn't seem possible. If anything, it wouldn't have surprised Elsa if some of her guests stormed out of the inn tonight in angry frustration.

But they didn't, and she thanks her wish capsule for that. As each wish was read, smiles were genuine; affection, moving ... in hand clasps and stolen kisses; words, subdued. Standing still this summer night, Elsa can almost hear slight echoes of it all in the salty breeze.

In a moment, Cliff is beside her, remarking on the special night she gave them. "The weekend's saving grace," he says, reaching an arm around her shoulders and giving a squeeze before turning to take down the paper lanterns. After that, he blows out all the candles except for the silver candle in her wish-happiness jar.

Which gets her to thinking of all the wishes read tonight. Still standing at the deck railing, she looks up at the smudged starlight on the misty night. What kinds of wishes have all those stars heard over time ... whispered with hope, pleaded with desperation, yearned for with love. Oh, if those stars could talk, the new constellations their stories might create.

Feeling the damp sea air, Elsa can't help but think of where Shane might be right now. Back in Maine? Already out on his beloved Atlantic Ocean on a lobster boat? Wearing that newsboy cap and a heavy sweatshirt against the sea spray? Or is he in a shingled fisherman's house by the docks, maybe? Most likely alone, hearing the low moan of a foghorn. With all those hazy stars over the distant water, she wonders what Shane could have possibly wished for this weekend. What hope did *he* have when he got in his truck two days ago and picked up the highway to Connecticut?

Behind her now, Cliff pours two glasses of wine, then sits and pulls out her chair. Before she joins him, Elsa vaguely blesses herself, as she does every night when she says a small prayer for Sal, gone a year now. Though most often she whispers the words while in bed, tonight it feels right to whisper them to the stars.

"*Dio ti benedica,*" she murmurs in Italian. "*God bless you, my sweet son.*"

She hesitates for a few long seconds. In the distance, gentle waves lap at the shore. For the first time then, Elsa repeats her prayer—this time for someone else.

For Shane Bradford, wherever the road took him earlier this morning. "*Dio ti benedica. God bless you … on your long journey, too.*"

thirty

Monday

THE SOUND OF THE GULLS crying out over the bluff wakes Jason at sunrise. The birds are raucous this morning. From his bed, he can just picture them swooping and dipping, on the hunt for fish, dropping crabs on the rocks. He waits a minute, eyes closed. But it's no use. Though it's early, today he can't fall back asleep.

So he quietly touches a strand of Maris' dark hair. Just for a moment. Then he turns, reaches for the forearm crutches leaning against his chair and gets out of bed. Even with the windows open, the air is still, and close. It'll be a hot day. So after rummaging through a couple of dresser drawers, he tucks a pair of cargo shorts and a short-sleeve button-down into a cloth bag hooked onto his crutches. Once in the bathroom, he hangs his clothes on a wall hook outside the tub, sets up his stool and turns on the spigot for a quick shower.

Night Beach

The odd thing is that during this past crazy weekend, it always felt like Monday would never arrive. The weekend was some sort of time warp, not moving the hands of the clock forward.

But once he's showered and back in the bedroom, rolling a silicone liner and sock onto his stump, Jason's well assured that time moved on. All it takes, after attaching his prosthetic left leg just below the knee, is one look at the planner app on his cell phone. Yup, the weekend is wiped clean as he reads his day's itinerary: design consultation at new White Sands Beach job; filming with CT-TV camera crew at Fenwick cottage to discuss proposed room layouts with Mitch, Carol and contractor overseeing reno; stop at salvage yard to pick up vintage viewfinder.

"*Fine, fine,*" Jason says under his breath. He clicks off the planner and goes downstairs to the kitchen. "*I'll get to it.*"

First things first, though. After a cup of coffee with a hefty slice of leftover wedding cake, an early sunrise walk with Maddy. The dog needs it. Jason needs it. He wants to get to the beach, take in the August quiet. Wants to be sure all is finally well in his small world.

Walking with Maddy along Sea View Road, the street is gritty with sand. To the east, the rising sun shines golden light on Long Island Sound. A motorboat and small cabin cruiser anchored there gently bob on the calm water.

But it's the beach Jason wants to see. Wants to walk. Especially on the packed sand just below the high tide line. There's no other place on this blessed earth that cradles his gait, cradles his thoughts, the way that strip of sand does.

Once on the boardwalk, he unleashes the German shepherd and lets her run along the driftline. Her nose to the dried seaweed, her tail wagging, she lopes down the beach.

The *empty* beach, this early on a Monday. No vacationers have stationed their sand chairs and umbrellas yet. No joggers run along the water. There is only that smooth sand, water and sky, giving him a clear view of the last-standing cottage near the rock jetty. Rising on stilts, the imposing gray house has always been the grande dame of Stony Point. What's hard to believe is that it's been only weeks since he signed on Mitch Fenwick and his daughter, Carol, to a televised renovation project.

Feels like a lifetime ago.

Already the initial Castaway Cottage episodes have been mapped, blueprints drawn, zoning variances filed. And soon after Labor Day weekend? Demo commences. It's not a total teardown, like the old Maggie Woods place—often referred to in these parts as the dump on the hill. No, the Fenwick cottage has history *worth* saving, worth preserving. So any demo work scheduled is only with the intent of enhancing the original structure.

Before all that, though, the film crew is due here to get sufficient footage of the before-shots. Good weather is predicted, so the taping should go smoothly. Jason walks past the lone cottage on the beach now. Waves lap along the shore; the sand is firm beneath his gait. Once he reaches the rocky ledge beyond, he lets Maddy slosh in the shallows there for a few minutes. While he waits, he looks at the

Fenwick cottage in the morning light, but *remembers* Mitch inviting him and Kyle inside in the dark of night—just two days ago. Did that really happen? Now it seems like a distant memory as workday routine gradually returns.

On his way back home, Jason stops on the dunes and snaps a few blossoms off the wild hydrangea bushes there. He'll give them to Maris, who he's sure will put them in their old fishing shack—the flowers inspiration for her writing as she settles in again with Neil's novel. Even the thought of *her* normal life resuming brings a sense of relief. Back in the cottage kitchen, he puts the hydrangeas in a vase and jots a note wishing Maris a nice writing day. Then he makes a sandwich for an early lunch, packs in a peach and, okay, another slab of cake before gathering together his design tablet and rough sketches, too.

Giving a look around the quiet kitchen, he grabs his cell phone and heads out, loading up his SUV with several blueprint tubes and a large gadget bag. Yes, the weekend's definitely over.

Still … Feeling like a sentry, he drives the winding Stony Point streets. After the past few days' utter turmoil, everything needs one last checking-up on. So he swings over to Bayside Road and cruises past the Bradfords' cottage. It's buttoned up tight while they're staying at that shanty in the woods, completely unplugged. Otherwise, Jason might have texted them a photo of their waiting house.

Next up? He turns onto Ridgewood Road and passes Beach Box. That tiny little reno is also scheduled to get underway once the Hammer Law's lifted the morning after Labor Day. Lord knows, when that Hammer Law's lifted, it's practically a holiday around here. Hammers, excavation vehicles, dump trucks, scaffolding, lumber deliveries, power saws, roof shingles, jackhammers, ladders—vehicles and equipment will be rising, swinging, banging, whirring. Dumped, unloaded and piled up.

But not yet.

Jason circles around the beach roads once more. He first drives past Matt and Eva's house on the marsh, then Elsa's inn. Only when he sees their vehicles parked in driveways, their house windows open, sun glinting on dewy lawns, is he satisfied that everyone's okay.

Actually? Driving the cottage-lined streets in the light of day now, the weekend feels like a mirage, if he had to name it. The painful details and memories are fading, almost like it never even happened.

―

But it happened, all right.

What Jason sees next proves it. Damn, it's just like he's always thought. Where Shane Bradford goes, so goes trouble.

And it looks like Shane didn't go far.

Up ahead, Jason first notices Shane's old seaworn, salt-coated pickup truck parked beside a little beach bungalow. The cottage is run-down, its shingles weathered, the cream trim paint peeling. Running through scrubby beach grass, there's a makeshift walkway built with old boardwalk planks. It leads from the driveway, along the side of the cottage, to an open rear porch overlooking Long Island Sound. Jason's got a clear view as he drives his SUV closer.

The problem is, as much as he wants to, he can't stop, or even slow too much. The last thing he needs is for Shane to notice him.

As he nears, though, Jason sees enough.

Enough to recall Elsa's story of Shane throwing his duffel onto the lobster boats. The thud of his duffel hitting the deck always marked the beginning of a new voyage. Of weeks ahead doing nothing more than lobstering. Of doing what he loves.

Because wouldn't you know it? Just then, Shane Bradford, standing in jeans and a tee behind his pickup, lifts his packed duffel from the truck bed, walks beside the cottage and throws that duffel. Lifts it right over his shoulder and hefts it through the air to land on the open back porch—the same way he must throw that duffel boarding a lobster boat.

Oh, and there's one more thing Jason notices as he passes the shabby little beach bungalow. Can't miss it, actually, as he cruises past. It's the *For Rent* sign propped in the cottage's front window.

"Son of a bitch," Jason whispers while throwing a glance back at the now-*rented* little beach bungalow.

Looks like Shane's voyage this time around landed him right here.

Right at an old shingled cottage with sea views.
Right in the midst of all their lives.
Right at Stony Point.

The beach friends' journey continues in

LITTLE BEACH BUNGALOW

The next novel in the Seaside Saga from New York Times Bestselling Author

JOANNE DEMAIO

Also by Joanne DeMaio

The Seaside Saga
(In order)
1) *Blue Jeans and Coffee Beans*
2) *The Denim Blue Sea*
3) *Beach Blues*
4) *Beach Breeze*
5) *The Beach Inn*
6) *Beach Bliss*
7) *Castaway Cottage*
8) *Night Beach*
9) *Little Beach Bungalow*
10) *Every Summer*
—And More Seaside Saga Books—

Summer Standalone Novels
True Blend
Whole Latte Life

Winter Novels
Eighteen Winters
First Flurries
Cardinal Cabin
Snow Deer and Cocoa Cheer
Snowflakes and Coffee Cakes

For a complete list of books by *New York Times* bestselling author Joanne DeMaio, visit:

Joannedemaio.com

About the Author

JOANNE DEMAIO is a *New York Times* and *USA Today* bestselling author of contemporary fiction. The novels of her ongoing and groundbreaking Seaside Saga journey with a group of beach friends, much the way a TV series does, continuing with the same cast of characters from book-to-book. In addition, she writes winter novels set in a quaint New England town. Joanne lives with her family in Connecticut.

For a complete list of books and for news on upcoming releases, please visit Joanne's website. She also enjoys hearing from readers on Facebook.

Author Website:
Joannedemaio.com

Facebook:
Facebook.com/JoanneDeMaioAuthor

Made in the USA
Monee, IL
26 May 2025

18214864R00163